Robur The Conqueror:

Master of the World

Robur The Conqueror:

Master of the World

BY

Jules Verne

Fredonia Books
Amsterdam, The Netherlands

Robur the Conqueror:
Master of the World

by
Jules Verne

ISBN: 1-4101-0072-3

Copyright © 2002 by Fredonia Books

Reprinted from the 1887 edition

Fredonia Books
Amsterdam, The Netherlands
http://www.fredoniabooks.com

Robur The Conqueror:

Master of the World

ROBUR THE CONQUEROR.

CHAPTER I.

IN WHICH BOTH THE SCIENTIFIC AND IGNORANT ARE NONPLUSED.

"BANG! Bang!"

The sound of two pistol shots was heard. A cow crossing a field fifty paces distant received a bullet in the spine.

The cow was an innocent victim. Like spectators at a riot she had fared worse than the combatants.

The contending adversaries were untouched.

Who were these adversaries?

All that could be gathered from their appearance was that the elder was an Englishman and the younger an American. The party were on the Canadian side of the Niagara River, about three miles below the falls and not far from the bridge which unites the opposite shores.

The Englishman crossed over to the American.

"I still maintain that it was 'Rule Britannia,'" said he.

"It was 'Yankee Doodle,'" replied the other.

The quarrel was about to commence again, when one of the seconds interposed, saying:

"Let us put it 'Rule Doodle' and 'Yankee Britannia,' and go to breakfast." This compromise between the national airs of America and Great Britain was adopted, to the general satisfaction of all concerned, and Americans and English crossed the bridge and were soon seated in the dining-room of the hotel. There, surrounded with the traditional ham and eggs, cold roast beef, incendiary pickles and floods of tea which rivaled the celebrated cataract, they ceased for a time to dispute on a subject in regard to which they still differed.

Who was right—the Englishman or the American? It would prove a difficult matter for any one to decide this question. But at all events the duel showed a phase of the excitement that was existing not only on the new, but on the old continent as well, concerning an inexplicable phenomenon which during the month past had baffled all attempts at explanation.

Never since the appearance of man on the terrestrial globe had the heavens been so closely scanned.

On the night preceding the encounter just recorded the notes of an aerial trumpet had sounded over that portion of Canada situated between Lake Ontario and Lake Erie. Some of the inhabitants had heard " Yankee Doodle " and the others " Rule Britannia," and from this had arisen the Anglo-American quarrel which had just ended in the breakfast at Goat Island.

Perhaps it had been neither of these patriotic airs, but it undoubtedly was the note of a trumpet, and possessed a striking singularity from the fact that the sound came from the sky toward the earth.

Could it possibly have been a celestial trumpet sounded by an angel or an archangel, or was it a party of happy aeronauts who amused themselves by blowing sonorous blasts over the wondering world?

No, it was neither angel nor aeronaut. An extraordinary phenomenon was being produced in the highest zones of the sky, a phenomenon whose origin and nature had baffled every one.

To-day it appeared over America, forty-eight hours later over Europe, eight days later in Asia, above the Celestial Empire. If this trumpeter, so loudly sounding his rapid flight, was not the announcer of the day of judgment, who, then, was he? At this time all the nations of the earth—kingdoms and republics—were beginning to be alarmed and disturbed.

If you were to hear in your own house strange and inexplicable noises, you would at once endeavor to discover the cause of disturbance, and failing, you would naturally abandon your house and dwell in another. But in this case the house was the terrestrial globe, and we possess no means of leaving it for the moon, Mars, Venus, Jupiter or any other planet of the solar system. All that remained was to discover what unusual occurrence was transpiring, not in infinite space, but in the atmospheric zones surrounding the earth. For, no air, no noise, and as there certainly was noise — always the famous trumpet—the phenomenon was, of course, transpiring within that strata of air, which, with a diminishing density, and a height of not more than six miles, surrounds our sphere.

All the newspapers naturally began to discuss the question, treating it in all its different aspects, throwing light on it or obscuring it, recapitulating stories true or false, alarming or reassuring their readers, and, in short, keeping the easily led masses in a state of continual excitement.

The observatories of the entire world were consulted. If they could not solve the riddle, of what use were observatories? If the astronomers, who could double and triple stars at a distance of three hundred million leagues, were unable to explain the origin of a cosmic phenomenon within the radius of a few miles, of what use were astronomers?

It would be impossible to estimate the number of eyes that during those beautiful summer nights were eagerly scanning the heavens through telescopes, field-glasses, lorgnettes and every other optical instrument as yet invented. Never had even an eclipse been greeted with so imposing a spectacle. The observatories replied, but insufficiently. Each of them gave a different opinion, and a scientific war waged during the last weeks of April and the first of May. The observatory of Paris exhibited considerable reserve and none of the sections pronounced on the problem. In the bureau of mathematical astronomy they disdained to consider it; in that of meridian operations nothing was discovered, and from the departments of meteorology and geodesy no light could be gained. In fact, among all these scientists not one would declare himself capable of throwing light on the subject. They at least were frank.

The news from the provinces was a little more affirmative. During the night from the 6th to the 7th of May there had appeared a light, of presumable electric origin, the duration of which was about twenty seconds. At Pioan-Midi this light was seen between the hours of nine and ten in the evening. At the meteorological observatory of Puy-de-Donne they perceived it about one or two in the morning; at Mont Ventoux, in Provence, between two and three o'clock; at Nice, between three and four; and in Semnoz-Alps, at Annecy, it showed itself just as day was breaking. It was impossible to reject these numerous observations, and the fact was established that the light had, during successive hours, been observed from the different posts. Whether this light was the focus of numerous reflections crossing the terrestrial atmosphere, or whether it was a single product, it possessed the power of moving with a rapidity of over two miles an hour.

But had nothing abnormal been observed in the air in daytime?

Nothing. The trumpet at least might have been heard through the strata of air, but, strange to say, between the rising and setting of the sun it was silent.

In Great Britain every one was perplexed and the observatories were unable to agree. Greenwich had heard the blast, Oxford had seen the light, but they both asserted that "it was nothing."

"Optical illusion!" said one.

"Acoustic illusion!" replied the other.

On the details of the phenomenon they disagreed, but they both declared it an illusion.

At the observatory of Berlin, and that of Vienna, the discussion threatened to cause international complications. But Russia, in the person of the director of the observatory of Poulkowu, proved to them that they were both right, as they had viewed the phenomenon from different points and consequently beheld different phases of it.

In Switzerland at the observatory of Sautis, at that of Appenzel, at Rigi, at the posts of Saint Gothard, Saint Bernard, Julier Simplon, Zurich, and at Zomblick in the Tyrolean Alps, the watchers at the telescopes were late in giving an opinion and could offer no new information.

But in Italy, at the meterological stations of Vesuvius, at the post of Etna, installed in the old Casa Inglese and at Monte Cava, the astronomers did not hesitate to admit the materiality of the phenomenon, declaring that they had discovered it during the daytime in the shape of a little scroll of vapor and at night under the appearance of a shooting star.

The mystery began to weary the men of science as much as it was terrifying the ignorant and lower class, who, thanks to one of the wisest laws of nature, constitute an immense majority in our world.

The astronomers and meteorologists were gradually dropping the question, and would have done so entirely, but for a new development of the mysterious case. The night from the 26th to the 27th at the observatory of Kantokeino, in Norway, and the night of the 28th to the 29th at that of Isfjord, in Spitzenberg, the Norwegians on one side and the Swedes on the other both agreed to this fact: The apparition of an aerial monster, with the form of a large bird and surrounded with an electric halo. It had not been possible to determine the structure of the monster, but they discovered that from time to time I threw out corpuscles, which exploded like bombs.

In Europe they showed some disposition to doubt this report from Norway and Spitzenberg. But it certainly had some foundation, as both the Swedes and Norwegians, who ordinarily were unable to agree on any point, seemed to be in perfect accord on this subject.

At the observatories of South America, in Brazil and Peru, and at those of Australia at Sidney, Adelaide and Melbourne they laughed at the pretended discovery.

Among all the scientists of the world only one astronomer dared to offer a practical solution of the mystery, in spite of the ridicule which his statement gave rise to. He was a Chinaman, the director of the observatory of Zi-Ka-Wey.

" The object in question is simply a flying machine."
What nonsense!

In the meantime, while the controversy was progressing vigorously in the Old World, it was being pushed to a further extent in the new, especially in the United States.

The observatories at Washington and at Cambridge were waging an astronomical war with those at Dartmouth College, in New Hampshire, and Ann Arbor, Michigan. The subject of their dispute was not the nature of the discovered body, but the precise moment of observation, for they each claimed to have seen it the same night, and at the same hour and the same minute. This was clearly folly, as the distance from Michigan to New Hampshire is too great to admit of simultaneous observation.

During the night of the 12th to 13th of May the astronomers at Yale College heard the sound of the famous trumpet and recognized note for note, rhythm for rhythm, the refrain of the Chant du Depart.

"Good!" replied the humorous papers. "It is a French orchestra practicing in the clouds."

"But joking is not solving," was the severe rejoinder of the Atlantic Iron Works Society of Boston, whose opinion on astronomical questions was law in the scientific world.

At last the observatory of Cincinnati, endowed in 1870 by Mr. Kilgore, of that city, came to the front. The director declared that on the previous night he had discovered a moving body which appeared at short intervals in different parts of the heavens, but the nature, dimensions and motive power of which it had been impossible to determine.

At this crisis the New York "Herald" received an anonymous communication which read as follows:

"The public has not forgotten the rivalry which existed a few years ago between the two heirs of the Begum of Ragginhara—the French doctor Sarrasin, in his town of Franceville, and the German inventor, Herr Schultze, in his town, Stahlstadt, both situated only a few miles apart in the southern part of Oregon. It will be remembered that Herr Schultze in an attempt to destroy Franceville discharged from a monster cannon a huge projectile intended to fall over the French town and annihilate it. The shot, through a miscalculation, was thrown with a rapidity sixteen times greater than that of ordinary projectiles, say five hundred leagues an hour, and did not refall on the earth, but is circulating and will circulate for eternity around our globe. It is probable that the supposed phenomenon is nothing but this material projectile."

Very ingenious, but how about the trumpet? Did Herr Schultze fire off a musician with his projectile? All these explanations failed to satisfactorily account for the phenomenon, and there remained nothing feasible but the hypothesis proposed by the director at Zi-Ka-Wey. But the opinion of a Chinaman— The dispute continued, and grew fiercer every day.

Four days elapsed, during which no one had been able to locate the mysterious object. Could it possibly have fallen in some place where it was unable to rise again, the sea for instance? Was it reposing in the depths of the Atlantic, Pacific or Indian Oceans? This disappearance was giving rise to numerous conjectures, when from the 2d to the 9th of June a series of facts were developed, the explanation of which was impossible, save by admitting the existence of a cosmic phenomenon.

During this short space of time the Turks at the highest minaret of Saint Sophie, the Rouonnais from the metal spire of their cathedral, the Americans from the head of the Statue of Liberty at the mouth of the Hudson, and from the Bunker Hill monument at Boston, the Chinese from the summit of the temple at Canton, the Hindoos in their temple at Tarjour, the Italians from the cross of the Cathedral of St. Peter's of Rome, the English at the cross of St. Paul in London, the Egyptians on the highest peak of the Grand Pyramid of Gizeh, and the Parisians at the top of the iron tower erected for the exposition in 1889, all saw in their turn a strange body which floated at ease around these almost inaccessible points. It resembled a pavilion of black silk studded with stars and a golden sun in the center.

CHAPTER II.

THE MEMBERS OF THE WELDON CLUB EXHIBIT A SLIGHT DIFFERENCE OF OPINION.

" No one can dispute it. "

" No! But we shall and do dispute it in spite of your threats!"

" Be careful what you say, Bat Fyn. "

" Take care yourself, Uncle Prudent. "

" I insist that the screw should be placed behind!"

" So do we! So do we!" responded fifty voices together.

" No; it should be in the front," cried Phil Evans.

" In front! In front!" shouted fifty voices no less vigorously.

" We still hold our convictions and always shall," replied the other fifty.

" Then what is the use of disputing?"

" It is not a dispute—it is a discussion. "

For a good quarter of an hour these retorts and vociferous yells had filled the drawing-room of the celebrated Weldon Club, situated on Walnut Street, in the city of Philadelphia.

On the night in question the inhabitants were on the eve of the election of a gaslighter; there had been public manifestations, excited meetings, and blows had even been exchanged between the members of the different parties. The members of the Weldon Club had doubtless participated in the struggle, and were still charged with the excitement. Their present meeting, however, was only a simple reunion of "balloonists," discussing a question which, to them, was most momentous, the steering or guiding of balloons. These proceedings were transpiring in a city whose rapid development had been more remarkable than any other American city, New York, Chicago, Cincinnati or San Francisco. A city which is neither a port, nor a mining or petroleum center—a city larger than either Berlin, Manchester, Edinburgh, Liverpool, Vienna, St. Petersburg or Dublin—a city which possesses a park larger than the seven parks of London combined, in short, a city which comprises over a million souls, and which is the fourth city of the world.

Philadelphia is almost a city of marble, and the magnificence of its houses and public edifices is unrivaled. The greatest of the colleges of the new continent is the Girard College, of Philadelphia. The largest iron bridge in the world is thrown across the Schuylkill River.

Freemasonry's most imposing and beautiful temple is undoubtedly the Masonic Temple at Philadelphia. And, last but not least, the largest association of adepts in aerial navigation was the Weldon Club, of Philadelphia.

A visit to the Weldon Club the night of the 12th of June would have been well worth the trouble. In the large hall

debating, struggling, gesticulating, discussing and dis
puting, were a hundred or more balloonists, under the
authority of a president, assisted by a secretary and a treasurer. They were not professional exhibitors, but simply
amateurs in everything that appertained to aerostatics,
but who vigorously opposed the introduction of flying
machines, aerial ships and other apparatus " heavier than
air."

It is possible, however, that the valiant members of
the Weldon Club were willing to admit the steering of balloons, but as regards any other manipulation they drew the
line.

The president, well known in Philadelphia, was the
famous Uncle Prudent—Prudent being his family name,
The prefix, Uncle, is not surprising in America, where one
can be uncle and have neither nephew nor niece.

Uncle Prudent was a personage of considerable importance, and in spite of his name was noted for his reckless-
ness. He was very rich, but this could hardly be called a
fault, even in the United States. Besides, how could he
help being wealthy, as he was the largest stockholder of the
Niagara Falls Company, a company formed for the utilization of the water passing over the falls. The seven thousand five hundred cubic feet of water that went over every
second produced a force equal to seven million horse
power. The revenue from the supply of this enormous
force to the manufactories within a circle of five hundred
miles gave a net profit to the company of some three million dollars a year, the larger part of which went into Uncle
Prudent's pockets.

Notwithstanding, he was frugal in his living and possessed but a single servant, his valet Frycollin, who was as timid as his master was audacious.

Uncle Prudent was rich, and that he had friends goes without saying; but he also had enemies, for he was president of the club, and there were a few who envied him his position. Among them the most implacable was Phil Evans, the secretary of the Weldon Club.

Phil Evans, in his antagonism was certainly not mercenary, for he was the head of the Walton Watch Company, a concern that makes five hundred watch movements a day, and whose workmanship is equal, if not superior, to the best Swiss productions. All that he needed to make him supremely happy was that envied position held by Uncle Prudent. They were both about the same age—forty-five, both possessed strong constitutions, both of undoubted courage, and each was inclined to believe that the state of bachelorhood possessed considerable more charms than that of wedlock.

Phil Evans and Uncle Prudent had both been candidates for the presidency of the club and each received the same number of votes. Twenty ballots were taken, which in every instance resulted in a tie.

It was an embarrassing situation and threatened to last as long as either of the candidates lived, but one of the members of the club proposed a means of settling the question.

It was Jem Cip, the treasurer, a confirmed vegetarian, one of that sect who proscribed all animal food and all fermented liquors, a rival of Niewman, Pitman, Ward,

Davies and other shining lights of that particular class of inoffensive lunatics.

Jem Cip was supported in his scheme by another member of the club, William T. Forbes, the proprietor of a large glucose manufactory, where sugar was made out of paper and old rags. He was a very sedate and dignified individual, and was the father of two charming young ladies, Miss Dorothy, commonly called Dollie, and Miss Martha, called Mat, who gave tone to the best society of Philadelphia.

Jem Cip's proposition, backed by William T. Forbes and some other members, was finally adopted, and it was decided to elect the president of the club by the " middle point." The fact is, this method of election had become so popular that there were a large number of Americans who advocated its employment in nominating the candidates for the position of President of the United States.

A long black line was drawn on each of two pieces of white paper. These two lines were precisely the same length, as they had been measured with mathematical exactitude. The papers were to be placed on two tables in the middle of the room and the two candidates each furnished with a fine needle. They were to approach their own table at the same time, and the candidate who planted his needle nearest the center of the line would be the acknowledged president of the Weldon Club.

Uncle Prudent planted his needle at the same time as Phil Evans sunk his. Measurements were taken to decide which had come nearest the center.

Again matters were brought to a standstill. The two

gentlemen had been so precise in their calculation that no
material difference could be detected between their measurements.

The room was in a state of excitement and uproar, and
it is impossible to say what might have happened had not
one of the members suggested a solution of the difficult
question. He insisted that the measurements be tested by
the gradual ruler, divided by the micrometer invented by
M. Perreaux, which was capable of dividing an inch into
fifteen hundred parts. His suggestion was adopted and
measurements retaken with the following result:

Uncle Prudent's mark was six five-hundredths of an
inch from the center, and that of Phil Evans nine five-
hundredths of an inch.

And this is why Phil Evans was only secretary of the
Weldon Club, and Uncle Prudent was the proclaimed
president.

It was but a small space of only three five-hundredths
of an inch, but it was the cause of filling Phil Evans with
a hate for his colleague which, though latent, was none the
less ferocious.

At this time some little progress had been made relative
to the guiding or steering of balloons. The attachment of
propellers and screws had been attempted in 1852 by Henry
Giffard, in 1872 by Dupuy de Lome, in 1883 by the Tissandier brothers, and in 1884 by Captains Krebs and
Renard. But if these machines in an atmosphere heavier
than themselves were capable of being steered by a propeller and of running against a light wind, it was owing to
the highly favorable circumstances attending the trial. In

a large hall, quiet and close, they were perfect, and in a calm atmosphere favorable results might be shown. But really nothing practical had been attained.

Against a light wind, eight feet to the second, these machines would rest almost stationary; against a fresh breeze, ten feet to the second, they would slowly retreat; in a storm, twenty-five feet a second, they would be carried along like a feather; in the middle of a tempest, forty-five feet to the second, they would run a chance of being broken to pieces, and in one of those cyclones, which attain a velocity of over a hundred feet a second, there would not be a trace left of the machine.

The limited experiments of Captains Krebs and Renard proved that this method of guiding balloons could only be employed in a calm atmosphere, and consequently would not admit of a practical application. One side of the problem—that of the means by which balloons might be guided—progressed, however, to a more advanced stage.

The steam propeller invented by Henry Giffard was supplanted by the use of electric motors.

The bichromate of potash batteries, which were used by the Tissandier brothers in their machine, were capable of imparting a speed of four feet a second. The electro-dynamos employed by Captain Renard developed a force of about fourteen horse power, giving a rapidity of at least six feet a second.

In this struggle of inventors endeavoring to discover a light and powerful motor the Americans came nearest to attaining the desired combination. An electric apparatus based on the use of a new battery, the composition of which was as yet unknown, had been purchased by the Weldon Club from the inventor, a chemist of Boston. Calculations made with the greatest care and diagrams executed with the greatest exactitude demonstrated that with this apparatus, driven by a propeller of suitable size, a speed of from eighteen to twenty feet a second might be produced. This invention was extraordinary.

"And it is not dear," Uncle Prudent had remarked, as he looked at the receipt for the last installment of one hundred thousand dollars, that he had just paid the inventor. The Weldon Club immediately applied itself to work. Whenever money is needed to develop a matter of practical utility the American pockets are quickly opened, and in this case the fund was quickly subscribed. Three hundred thousand dollars came promptly from the members of the club at the first call. The work commenced at once under the supervision of the most celebrated aeronaut of the United States, Harry W. Tinder, immortalized by the three most daring ascensions on record. In the first of these, he had risen to a height which almost doubled that attained by either Gay-Lussac, Coxwell, Sivel, Tissandier or Spinelli. In the second he crossed the United States, from New York to San Francisco, surpassing the trips made by Nadar, Godard or any one else, excepting John Wise.

The third trip had been terminated by a frightful fall of fifteen hundred feet, which only resulted in a slight sprain, while De Rosier, less fortunate, only fell from a height of seven hundred feet, and, landing on his head, was instantly killed. The Weldon Club pushed the work forward vigorously, and in a short time a monster balloon floated in a field in the suburbs of the city. The operation of testing had been performed by filling it with air, under a strong pressure, and it stood the trial nobly and proved worthy of the title monster. The balloon owned by the celebrated John Wise had a capacity of twenty thousand cubic feet, and the Giffard balloon twenty-five thousand cubic feet. Compare these two balloons with that of the one just constructed by the Weldon Club, containing forty thousand cubic feet, and you will admit that Uncle Prudent and his colleagues might be pardoned for swelling with pride.

This balloon was not intended to explore the highest strata of the air, and consequently was not called "Excelsior," a name which stands high in favor among the Americans. It was named the "Go Ahead," and all that remained was for it to prove itself worthy of the name by obeying every command of its captain.

In six weeks the "Go Ahead" would take its first flight through space. It has been seen that all the details of the mechanism had not as yet been thoroughly decided upon. Meetings of the club had been called to discuss, not the shape nor dimensions of the propeller, but whether it should be placed in the rear of the apparatus, like that used by the Tissandier brothers, or in front like the one employed by Captains Krebs and Renard. The partisans of each system were unable to effect a compromise, and even came to blows. The "Frontites" comprised fifty members, and the "Rearites" possessed the same number of adherents.

As long as this state of affairs continued it was impossible to adjust the propeller.

Unless the government should interfere all operations might remain as they stood for an indefinite period of time. But in the United States the government does not meddle with private affairs or things that do not concern it.

With matters in this state, the meeting on the night of the 13th of June threatened to end in a riot—threats exchanged, blows following threats and revolvers succeeding blows—when at eight o'clock something occurred to attract the attention of the members.

One of the ushers of the club crowded his way through the stormy meeting to the president's desk, and handing him a card, waited for any orders that might be given in return. Uncle Prudent read the card and turned the valve of the steam whistle which served to call the meeting to order, but the tumult continued unabated. Then Uncle Prudent resorted to an extreme measure.

He took off his hat. The sight of a fellow-citizen standing inside a house with his hat off startled the members into silence.

"A communication," said Uncle Prudent, taking an enormous pinch from the snuff-box at his side.

"Read it!" shouted ninety-nine voices, forgetting in the excitement to disagree.

"My friends, a stranger asks the privilege of being introduced into our meeting to-night."

"Never!" replied all the voices.

"He desires to prove to us that to believe in the steering of balloons is to believe in the most absurd of all fallacies," said Uncle Prudent. A general howl followed this declaration.

"Bring him in! Bring him in!"

"What is the name of this singular personage?" asked the secretary, Phil Evans.

"Robur," replied Uncle Prudent.

"Robur! Robur!" shouted the members, and they impatiently awaited the new-comer's appearance.

CHAPTER III.

A NEW PERSONAGE INTRODUCES HIMSELF.

"CITIZENS of the United States, my name is Robur, and I am proud of it. Notwithstanding my youthful appearance, I am forty years of age, possess an iron constitution, considerable muscular force, and a stomach which would be accounted excellent, even in the country of ostriches. So much for my physical qualities."

This extraordinary speech was listened to in silence. Was this person a fool, or was he amusing himself at their expense? Not a murmur came from the meeting, which a short time before had been in a state of confusion and uproar. It was, however, only the calm before the storm. Robur's appearance justified him in claiming the qualities he had enumerated. He was of medium height, with squarely built shoulders supporting a robust neck, and a large head. His head, indeed, might easily be compared to the head of a bull, but of a bull with an intelligent face.

Between the eyes, which flashed angrily at the least con-

tradiction, there was a permanent contraction of the eye-
brows, a sign of great energy. A powerful chest, which
rose and fell like a blacksmith's bellows. His hands,
arms, limbs and feet were in proportion with his body.
Neither mustache nor whiskers, but a sailor's beard, which
exposed to view the masticatory muscles of a powerful jaw.
It has been calculated—is there anything that has not been
calculated?—that the muscles of the jaw of a crocodile are
capable of exerting a pressure equal to that of four hundred atmospheres, while those of a large dog only develop
about one hundred. From these facts the following curious formula has been constructed: If a pound of dog produces eight pounds of masticatory force, a pound of crocodile produces twelve. Well, a pound of Robur would have
produced about ten. He was, therefore, a medium between a dog and a crocodile.

It would be difficult to conjecture or guess Robur's nationality. He expressed himself in correct English without the nasal accent which distinguishes Americans, more
particularly the inhabitants of the New England states.

He continued:

"You see before you an inventor whose moral qualities
are in nowise inferior to his physical. I am afraid of no
person nor thing. and my will has never yielded to any
one. When I fix on a purpose all America, the entire
world may unite in vain to prevent me from attaining my
end. In my ideas and assertions I allow no contradiction.
I trouble you with these details, gentlemen, because it is
necessary that you should thoroughly understand my char-
acter from the start.

"Perhaps I am speaking too long of myself, but no
matter. And, now, think twice before you interrupt me,
for I am here to tell you things which will probably not
please you to hear."

"Proceed, honorable stranger," said Uncle Prudent,
whose curiosity had conquered him.

Robur apparently took no notice whatever of his audit-
ors, and began:

"After ages of attempts which have ended in failures,
and of trials which have resulted in nothing, there are still
to be found people so ignorant and feeble-minded as to still
believe in the direction of balloons. They imagine that
some motor, electric or steam, can be applied to their balloon toys in such a way as to enable them to resist the currents of air.

"They fancy that they can be masters of a balloon, as
one is master of a ship gliding over the surface of the seas.
Because some inventors have, in a still and calm atmosphere, succeded, they believe that the direction of aerial
machines lighter than air is practical. Nonsense. Here
before me to-night are a hundred of you who implicitly
believe in the realization of your dreams, and who are
throwing away thousands of dollars, not into water, but
into space.

"Well, you are struggling with the impossible!"

Were the members of the Weldon Club deaf? During
this sarcastic address they had not stirred. Probably they
were restraining themselves to see how far this audacious
contradictor would dare to go.

Robur continued:

"A balloon, a toy! To raise the weight of a pound, you must allow a whole cubic foot of gas. Have you ever thought while dreaming of resisting a current of wind with your trivial mechanism that the pressure exerted against the sails of a vessel is not less than four hundred horse power? Or that in the accident at the Tay Bridge the pressure of the wind reached four hundred and forty pounds to the square inch? Why, the very shape of your balloons is directly antagonized to the flying system of nature; they are neither supplied with the wings of a bird, nor the membranes of certain fish or certain mammalians."

"Animals with wings?" cried one of the members of the club.

"Yes; the bat, if I am not mistaken, has wings. Perhaps the gentleman thinks that the bat is a bird, but I have never heard of an omelet of bat eggs."

This settled all further interruption from that particular quarter, at least, and Robur continued his argument:

"Do not understand me to say that because of these failures man should renounce the conquest of the air and desist from his attempts to revolutionize the habits and manners of the world by the utilization of this admirable method of locomotion.

"Not at all. Man is master of the seas, thanks to the aid of vessels, oars, sails, screws and wheels, and he will also master atmospheric space by the use of machines heavier than air, for, although you will not admit it, it is absolutely necessary for them to be heavier to be stronger than air."

This time the meeting broke out. Cries and epithets from every quarter fell around Robur like shots from a gun. There had been a true declaration of war cast into the balloonist camp.

Robur did not move a muscle, but with his arms folded across his breast, calmly waited for silence.

Uncle Prudent, by a gesture, called the meeting to order.

"The future exploration of the heavens will be accomplished by flying machines, and not balloons. The air is a practically solid body, to penetrate which it is only necessary to displace a certain portion of it and with sufficient rapidity."

This theory, advanced by Robur, had been offered before him by the partisan of aerostats, whose work was slowly but surely leading to a solution of the problem.

Landelle, Nadar, Luzy, Liais, Babinet, Temple, Villeneuve, Tatin, Edison and a score of others had all laid down the same simple principle.

Robur remained undisturbed by the clamor which was arising around him, and concluded by saying:

"In your pretended art of ballooning you have done nothing, you have arrived at nothing, and you have dared nothing. The most intrepid of all your aeronauts, John Wise, who has performed an aerial journey of fourteen hundred miles, has renounced his project of crossing the Atlantic. In short, you have not advanced a single step in your science."

"Sir," said the president, vainly endeavoring to be calm, "you forget the words used by our immortal Franklin, at the time the first balloon was born, ' It is only an infant, but it will grow,' and it has grown."

" Allow me to contradict you, Mr. President. It has not grown, it has only enlarged, which is not the same thing."

Here was a direct attack on the plans of the Weldon Club, who had conceived, sustained and subscribed to the construction of a monster balloon. The room was filled with a mass of frantic and enraged members, threatening, gesticulating and surging like the waves of the ocean.

" Put him out!"

" Throw him out of the window and see if he is heavier than air."

But where there is much smoke there is little fire, and no one offered personal violence to the speaker, and as the voices subsided Robur's voice was again heard:

" The future progress will not be in the art of ballooning, my friends, it will be in flying apparatus. The bird flies, and it is not a balloon; it is a work of mechanism."

" Yes, it flies," cried Bat Fyn, almost bursting with rage, " but it flies contrary to all mechanical laws."

" Indeed," replied Robur, shrugging his shoulders, " I must differ with you, for whether it is the subject of flight, or any other operation, it is always safe to imitate nature, for she is never wrong. Between the albatross who gives hardly ten strokes of the wing a minute, the pelican who gives ninety—"

" Ninety-one," cried a bantering voice.

" And the bee, who gives one hundred and eighty a second—"

"One hundred and eighty-two," cried the same voice.

"The gnat with three hundred and thirty—"

"Three hundred and thirty and a half."

"And the mosquito, which strikes the air almost a thousand times a second—"

"Make it a million," cried the mocker.

But Robur proceeded with his demonstration, undisturbed by these interruptions.

"Between these different figures it is possible to strike a medium which will go far toward aiding us in the solution of our problem. The day that De Lucy established the fact that the beetle, an insect whose weight is only about two pennyweight, was able to carry in his flight a weight of over four hundred pennyweight, more than two hundred times his own weight, that day the problem of aerial navigation was solved. Moreover, it has also been clearly demonstrated that the size of the wing decreases in proportion as the dimensions and weight of the bird or insect increases. With this model before us it is possible to construct more than sixty different forms of flying apparatus—"

"Which can not fly," cried Phil Evans.

"Which can and will fly," continued Robur, undisturbed by the interruption, "and which will be the means of rendering man master of space."

"But what of the propeller?" replied Phil Evans. "A bird is not supplied with a propeller, as we all know, and yet you claim it as a model."

"It has been demonstrated by Monsieur Penaud," answered Robur, "that the action of the wings of a bird performing the operation of flight is precisely the same movement as that of a screw. The motor of the future will be the propeller and your balloons will be superseded and forgotten."

Again the uproar and confusion commenced and was prolonged for a short time, when, Uncle Prudent, profiting by a momentary calm, said:

"Proceed, you can speak here without fear of interruption."

It seems that the honorable president did not call these cries, retorts and yells interruptions, but simply an exchange of arguments. Uncle Prudent continued:

"But if you will allow me, I would remind you that the theory which you are supporting has been condemned and discarded by the greater part of all the inventors, both of America and of foreign countries as well. It is a system which has led to the death of Sarrasin Volant at Constantinople, of Voador at Lisbon, of Letur, Groof and many others whose names I have forgotten, to say nothing of Icarus, of mythological fame."

"This system," retorted Robur, "is no more censurable than that of ballooning, whose list of martyrs comprises the names of De Rozier, Madame Blanchard, of Donaldson and Grimwood, who were precipitated into Lake Michigan, of Sivel, Spinelli, Eloy, and a number of others whose names you take great pains to forget."

This was tit for tat.

"Besides," continued Robur, "with your balloons, which you imagine to be so perfect, you have never been able to attain a practical speed. It would take you ten years to make the tour around the world, while a flying machine would easily do it in eight days."

Fresh cries of protestation and denial arose at this bold statement, and the voice of Phil Evans was heard to speak.

"You are praising so highly the benefits of flying; have you ever attempted the feat?"

"I have."

"And you have made a conquest of the air?"

"Possibly."

"Hurrah for Robur the Conqueror!" shouted an ironical voice.

"Yes, Robur the Conqueror. I accept the name and will bear it, as I have the right."

"Permit us to doubt it!" cried Jem Cip.

"Gentlemen," replied Robur, whose brows were beginning to contract, "when I am seriously discussing a serious subject I do not allow my argument to be broken in upon by lunatics, and I should be happy to know the name of the gentleman who has just interrupted me."

"My name is Jem Cip, and I am a vegetarian."

"Citizen Cip," said Robur, "vegetarians as a rule have stomachs longer than those of other men, possibly a foot or more. You are, therefore, thin enough, and I trust you will not compel me to lengthen you out still further by commencing at your ears."

"Throw him out!"

"Tear him in pieces!"

"To the street with him!"

"Lynch him!"

"Make a propeller out of him!"

The fury of the balloonists had now reached the highest pitch, and they rushed from their seats and closed round the platform, where Robur was standing as unconcerned and as collected as a statue.

In vain did Uncle Prudent turn on the shrieking blast of the presidential steam-whistle. Suddenly the mass of infuriated members made a backward movement.

Robur had drawn his hands from his pockets, and pointing toward the excited crowd were two revolvers, and as Jem Cip, who was in the front rank, looked into the barrels of the weapons, he wondered whether vegetables grew in the other world.

Profiting by the retreat of his assailants and the silence that followed, Robur said:

"I am now certain that it was not Amerigo Vespucius who discovered the New World. It was Sebastian Cabot. Citizen balloonists, you are not Americans, you are cabbage-heads."

At this instant four or five pistol shots sounded through the room, but no one was hit.

The room was filled with smoke, and when it had cleared away all traces of the stranger had disappeared. Robur the Conqueror had flown away.

CHAPTER IV.

UNCLE PRUDENT AND PHIL EVANS CONTINUE THE ARGU MENT.

AT the close of the stormy meetings which, for some time past, had been nightly held at the Weldon Club, the members leaving the club-house filled Walnut Street and the immediate neighborhood with the noise and clamor of their protracted arguments, and the citizens living in the vicinity had more than once complained to the authorities of the noisy discussions which were held on their very doorsteps. The police had even been called upon to clear the streets to allow passers-by, who were totally indifferent to the subject of aerial navigation, to reach their homes.

But never before that night had the tumult assumed such large proportions, never had the neighbors more cause for complaint, never had the intervention of police been more necessary. The members of the Weldon Club had, however, some excuse for their excitement. They had been defied, their balloon laughed at, and one of their number, Jem Cip, insulted; and at the very time they were about treating the intruder as he deserved he had disappeared. Now they cried for vengeance. If they allowed the injury to pass unpunished, they were unworthy of the American blood that flowed through their veins. Amerigo Vespucius deposed in favor of Sebastian Cabot. Was not this last insult the more unpardonable because it was historically true? The members of the club poured out into Walnut Street and woke up the people for squares around, searching their houses and cellars, but in vain.

No trace of Robur could be found. After an hour they gave it up and separated for their respective dwellings, swearing to continue their search into every corner of the continent.

At twelve o'clock the neighborhood had become comparatively quiet, and the good citizens of Philadelphia plunged again into the slumber which is the enviable privilege of cities which are fortunate in not being manufacturing centers. The members of the club were seeking their dwellings, and some were already in bed, fast asleep. Jem Cip, who had been publicly accused of possessing a foot more stomach than the average human being, had found a restaurant, where he was regaling himself with his favorite vegetable soup. Two of the most influential balloonists, two only, did not appear desirous of returning to their houses so soon. They were taking advantage of the occasion by arguing with more than usual acrimony. They were the irreconcilable Uncle Prudent and Phil Evans, the president and the secretary of the Weldon Club.

At the door of the club-house, the valet, Frycollin, was waiting for Uncle Prudent, his master, and as the adversaries came out he followed them, without troubling himself concerning the subject of their argument.

They were disputing with a warmth which was increased by the spirit of rivalry which existed between them.

"No, sir," repeated Phil Evans, "if I had had the honor of presiding over the meeting of the Weldon Club to-night it would not have been the scene of such a scandal."

"And what would you have done if you had presided?" demanded Uncle Prudent.

"I would have cut short the words of that public insulter before he had even opened his mouth."

"It seems to me that in order to cut short his words it would be at least necessary to let him speak."

"Not in America, sir; not in America."

And, bandying words and exchanging threats, the two men walked along the deserted streets, which led them further from their homes at every step they took.

Frycollin followed at a short distance, trembling with fear as they entered the deserted avenue and turned suspicious-looking corners.

The darkness of the night was profound, and the moon, rising over the house-tops, was commencing to throw fantastic shapes around the pedestrians, and as the valet timorously peered into the darkness around him, he fancied he could see five or six shapes which seemed to be following their footsteps and dogging them around every corner.

Instinctively Frycollin crept nearer to his master, but he did not dare to break in on the excited argument which was in progress. The street along which they were walking was, without their being aware of it, leading them into Fairmount Park. During the height of their argument they were crossing the bridge over the Schuylkill River at Girard Avenue, and they found themselves in the midst of the vast tract of rolling turf and beautiful trees which forms the greatest park in the world.

Here the terrors of the valet increased, and with reason, for he could see the six shadows gliding over the bridge in their rear, and in the water below he fancied he could catch a glimpse of the reflection of six devils crossing a shadowy bridge. The pupils of his eyes dilated, and his body trembled like a leaf.

The valet Frycollin was a perfect poltroon.

A true South Carolina negro, about twenty-one years old, with an enormous head and a slender body. A clown, glutton, sluggard, and above all a superb coward. He had been in Uncle Prudent's service for three years, and would have quit it a hundred times had he not feared a worse.

Associated with the life of a master who was always ready to engage in the most daring enterprises, Frycollin found himself in many situations where his cowardice had been severely tested. But then his position had its advantages, and to him they were great ones. He was allowed to eat as much and sleep as long as he pleased. Frycollin should have remained in Boston, in the service of a certain Sneffel family, who were on the point of making a tour of Switzerland, but abandoned their plan on reading of an avalanche in that country.

That was the house of Frycollin, not that of Uncle Prudent.

Ah! Frycollin, if you could only have read the future!

Uncle Prudent had become accustomed to the failings of his servant, but he found in him one good quality, which atoned for all his other faults. Although Frycollin was a negro, he spoke without that odious jargon which is the distinguishing characteristic of the American negro.

But Frycollin was a coward, and, as the saying goes,
" as cowardly as the moon."

It is no more than just to protest against this insulting
reflection on blonde Phœbe, mild Selene, the chaste sister
of radiant Apollo. What right have we to accuse with
cowardice a planet who, ever since our world was a world,
has looked us in the face, and never once turned its back.

But be this as it may, at this time—it was long after
midnight—the pale orb was commencing to disappear in
the west behind the highest branches of the park trees,
and the shadows of the woods were becoming darker and
deeper. The trembling valet cast another frightened
glance around.

" Ugh, there they are again," said he, " and they are
coming nearer."

He could restrain himself no longer, and he sprung to
his master's side.

" Master Uncle?"

This was how the president of the Weldon Club had
wished to be called.

The dispute between the two rivals had now reached its
highest point, and as they excitedly circled around each
other Frycollin was making frantic endeavors to keep close
to their sides.

Completely absorbed in the argument they were plun-
ging deeper and deeper into the deserted depths of Fairmount Park, leaving far behind them the Schuylkill River
and the bridge leading to the city.

The three men found themselves in the midst of a forest
of trees, through the tops of which the moon was sending

its last pale rays. At the end of this forest opened out a large glade, a vast oval field, which would have been especially adapted for the uses of a racing track. No irregularity of ground would have broken the horses' gallop, not a tree would have obstructed the view of the spectators around this circular track of several miles. If Uncle Prudent and Phil Evans had not been so deeply absorbed in their dispute they would have noticed that the usual aspect of this particular portion of their familiar park was changed.

In the dark shadow at the other side of the opening was a strange-looking object, more like an inverted wind-mill than anything else. But neither the president nor the secretary of the Weldon Club seemed to notice either the strange object or the change that had been produced in this part of the park.

Frycollin could see the shapes no longer. They seemed to have stationed themselves in the shadow around the glade.

The valet was now in a pitiful condition, convulsed with fear, his limbs paralyzed, his hair standing erect. In short, he was in the last stages of fright.

His trembling knees refused to support him, and he gathered courage to cry for the last time:

" Master Uncle! Master Uncle!"

" What do you want?" replied Uncle Prudent.

Phil Evans and his rival would probably have eased the load of superfluous rage they were carrying by eventually thrashing the unfortunate valet, but they had no time.

A shrill whistle sounded through the wood, and the dark glade was suddenly illuminated with the dazzling glare of electricity. The thought instantly flashed through their minds that they were in an ambush and that the whistle was the signal for some act of violence. In shorter space of time than it takes to tell it six men had bounded across the open space, two on Uncle Prudent, two on Phil Evans and two on the valet Frycollin. The last two had a sinecure, as the negro was incapable of defending himself.

The president and secretary, taken by surprise by the suddenness of the attack, seemed to resist, but were powerless in the hands of their assailants.

In a few seconds they were gagged, blindfolded, bound hand and foot, and rapidly carried across the clearing. Their first thought was that they had fallen into the hands of a band of highwaymen, who had found the deserted recesses of the park a convenient spot in which to ply their nefarious occupation.

But, although Uncle Prudent had on his person several thousand dollars in bank-notes, they were not searched; and it was, therefore, necessary to abandon the theory of robbers.

Not a word had been spoken by these strange beings; and the next moment Uncle Prudent, Phil Evans and Frycollin felt themselves gently deposited—not on the grass of the clearing, but on a sort of platform, which seemed to tremble with their weight.

They heard a door close and the grating of a key in a lock told them that they were prisoners.

At this moment the vibration of the platform on which

they were resting increased, and a strange whir was heard in the calm of the night.

The next morning the city of Philadelphia woke into a state of confusion and excitement. They read in the morning papers an account of the events that had transpired the night before, at the meeting of the Weldon Club, the appearance of a mysterious personage who called himself Robur—Robur the Conqueror!—his attack on the scientific principles of the Balloon Club, of Philadelphia, and his inexplicable disappearance. This alone was sufficient cause to throw the good citizens into a state of excitement, but when they learned that during the night the president and secretary of the Weldon Club had also disappeared, the confusion was increased.

Searches were instantly instituted throughout the city and suburbs, but to no purpose. Every nook and corner of the great city were explored and overhauled, but no traces of the missing citizens could be discovered. The newspapers of Philadelphia, then those throughout the State of Pennsylvania, and later the entire press of the United States took up the subject and offered hundreds of theories, none of which led to any practical clew. Handbills and posters were scattered throughout the country offering considerable rewards, not only to any one who would find the lost men, but for any trace of their whereabouts as well. But the rewards remained unclaimed. If the earth had opened and swallowed the president and secretary of the Weldon Club their traces could not have been more effectually obliterated.

The Republican papers seized the opportunity to de-

mand that the strength of the police force be increased,
thereby to prevent an occurrence of a misfortune which
might fall to any citizen venturing out of his house after
dark, and they were right.   It is true that the opposition
papers declared that the proposed increase was unwise, as
unless a similar outrage was attempted it would be impossible to discover the authors of the present one, and possibly they were also right.   In the meantime the police
force remained unchanged.

CHAPTER V.

A SUSPENSION OF HOSTILITIES IS AGREED UPON BETWEEN
THE PRESIDENT AND THE SECRETARY OF THE WEL
DON CLUB.

A BANDAGE across their eyes, a gag between their teeth,
their hands and feet tightly bound, unable to see, speak or
move, Uncle Prudent, Phil Evans, and the valet Frycollin found themselves in an uncomfortable situation.   The
mental condition of the three men was also decidedly un-
pleasant.   Unable to guess who their assailants were, or
why they had been thrown like bags into a wagon, ignorant of their whereabouts or the fate that was reserved for
them.   This would have exasperated even a cow, and the
members of the Weldon Club can not reasonably lay claim
to possessing the patience of that useful animal.

It will be imagined that Uncle Prudent's ordinary violence was now worked up to the highest pitch.   Both he

and Phil Evans were doubtless thinking that it would be difficult for them to take their accustomed seats the next night at the meeting of the Weldon Club.

It is impossible to conjecture Frycollin's thoughts as he lay there gagged and blindfolded. He seemed more dead than alive. For an hour the situation of the prisoners remained unchanged. No one appeared to give them that liberty of movement and speech of which they were so much in need. They were reduced to stifled sighs and muttered oaths, forced through the gags in their mouths, and at intervals they struggled frantically in their efforts to loose the cords which bound them. After a few ineffectual attempts they lapsed into a quiet state. Since they were deprived of the sense of sight they were trying with the aid of the sense of hearing to gain some knowledge of their surroundings. But it was all useless, as they could hear nothing but the continual and inexplicable whir which seemed to vibrate in the very air around them.

At last something happened. Phil Evans had been quietly and calmly working at the cords which bound his wrists. Little by little the knot stretched, and gliding his fingers out, one after another, he at last obtained the freedom of his hands.

A vigorous rubbing restored the circulation, which had been obstructed by the cords, and the next moment Phil Evans had raised the bandage from his eyes, torn out the gag, and cut with his bowie-knife the cords which bound his feet. An American who did not possess a bowie-knife was a freak.

Phil Evans had only gained the power of moving and

speaking. That was all. His eyes were too weak from
the long confinement to be of any service to him, even in
the half obscurity of the cell around him. The single ray
of light came through a sort of loop-hole cut about seven
or eight feet up the wall.

Phil Evans instantly applied himself to the liberating of
his rival. A few strokes of the bowie-knife sufficed to cut
the cords which bound the enraged Uncle Prudent, who,
as soon as he had reached his feet and torn off the bandage
and gag, said in a half-strangled voice:

"Thanks!"

"Not at all," replied his colleague.

"Phil Evans?"

"Uncle Prudent?"

"Let us have here neither president nor secretary of the
Weldon Club."

"You are right," replied Phil Evans.

"Here are only two men seeking to avenge themselves
on a third, who shall be severely punished. And this
third—"

"Is Robur!"

"Is Robur!"

At last! Here was a subject on which the two ex-dis-
putants could agree. On this subject there was no fear of
argument.

"And your valet," observed Phil Evans, pointing to
Frycollin, who was snorting like a walrus, " shall I release
him?"

"Not yet," replied Uncle Prudent. "He will only

smother us with his cries, and we have something else to attend to at present."

"And that is—"

"To save ourselves, if it is possible."

"And even if it is impossible."

"You are right, Phil Evans, even if it is impossible."

The president and his colleague had not doubted for a moment that their capture had been the work of the strange man who called himself Robur. Simple and honest thieves would have first relieved them of their watches, jewelry and pocket-books, and then have cut their throats and thrown them over the bridge into the Schuylkill below. Instead of this, their property had been undisturbed, and they were imprisoned—in what? A grave question, that was necessary to be solved, before their preparations for escape could be attended with any chance of success.

"Phil Evans," said Uncle Prudent, "it would have been much better for us had we given our attention to the neighborhood into which we were wandering and less to the exchange of useless arguments. If we had remained in the streets of Philadelphia this thing would not have happened. This Robur was evidently aware of what was transpiring at the club, and foresaw the disturbance that his antagonistic attitude raised, and to protect himself he very properly placed several of his bandits within call. When we left Walnut Street these scoundrels followed us, and when we imprudently lost ourselves in the depths of Fairmount Park we were at their mercy."

"Of course," replied Phil Evans. "Yes, we should have gone directly to our homes."

"We all can generally tell what we should have done after the matter is all over," answered Uncle Prudent.

At this moment a long sigh came from the darkest corner of the cell.

"What was that?" asked Phil Evans.

"Nothing, only Frycollin dreaming!" And Uncle Prudent continued: "Between the moment we were seized, a few steps from the clearing, and the time we were thrown into the cell, there was only a space of about two minutes' time. It is, therefore, evident that we are still in Fairmount Park."

"And if the cell had been moved we would certainly have felt it," said the secretary.

"Of course," replied Uncle Prudent. "We are doubtless imprisoned in a compartment of a large wagon or some other vehicle, and as we have felt no movement we must still be in the clearing. Now is the time for us to make our escape and seek this Robur later."

"He shall pay dearly for this attack on the liberty of two American citizens."

"Very dearly!"

"But who is this man? From what country does he come? Is he an Englishman, a German, or a Frenchman?"

"He is a wretch, and that is sufficient," replied Uncle Prudent. "Now to work."

With their hands stretched out and fingers open they felt carefully along the walls of the room, trying to find a joint of a crack. Nothing, not even at the door. It was hermetically closed, and the lock resisted all their attempts. It was necessary to cut a hole in the wall; and the question was whether their bowie-knives were strong enough for this work, or whether they would break and leave them helpless.

"Where does this ceaseless vibration come from?" said Phil Evans, surprised at the continued whir, which still sounded about them.

"It is probably the wind," answered Uncle Prudent.

"The wind? Up to midnight it seemed to me that the night was perfectly calm."

"Possibly so, Phil Evans. But if it is not the wind, what then is it?"

Phil Evans having opened the best blade of his knife tried to cut a hole in the wall near the door in the hope of making an opening large enough to allow the opening of the door from the outside, if it was closed with a bolt, or if the key had been left in the lock. Some minutes' hard work resulted in the breaking of the blade of the knife.

"This is of no use, Phil Evans."

"No."

"Can we be in a sheet-iron cell?"

"No, Uncle Prudent. These walls, when struck, do not give a metallic sound."

"Of iron-wood, then?"

"No, neither iron nor wood."

"What is it, then?"

"It is impossible to tell, but, at all events, it is a substance on which steel makes no impression."

Uncle Prudent was seized with a violent fit of rage, and kicked frantically at the unyielding door, while his hands endeavored to strangle an imaginary Robur.

"Be calm, Uncle Prudent," said Phil Evans; "be calm, try and see if you can do anything."

Uncle Prudent tried, but his knife could make no impression on a wall which snapped blade after blade as easily as if they were crystal instead of steel. All their attempts at flight were futile, and for a short while they desisted and awaited for any chance that might occur to escape. But it was not without objurgations and violent invectives addressed to Roburt; yet, considering his calm and unmoved demeanor during the excited meeting of the Weldon Club, it was not likely that these threats would have disturbed him.

In the meantime Frycollin was beginning to give unmistakable symptoms of illness. Whether he had cramps in the stomach or cramps in the limbs, he was struggling in a painful manner. Uncle Prudent thought it wise to put an end to these gymnastic exercises by cutting the cord which bound the negro.

But he soon repented his folly. The valet's release was attended with an interminable litany, in which the agony of fright was mingled with the pangs of hunger. Frycollin's brain was as weak as his stomach was strong, and it is hard to tell which of the two organs was now suffering the most.

"Frycollin!" cried Uncle Prudent.

"Master Uncle! Master Uncle!" responded the negro, between two lugubrious wails.

"It is possible that we are condemned to die of hunger in this prison. But we have resolved not to succumb until we have exhausted every means of alimentation capable of sustaining life."

"What—eat me!" cried the terrified valet.

"What else would one do with a negro in such a case?"

Frycollin began to seriously believe that he was to be employed in prolonging the life of the secretary and the president, and the agony of terror which the thought threw him into was painful. Time passed by, and all attempts to force the door or wall were futile. It was impossible to recognize the composition of the wall. It was neither metal, wood, nor stone. The floor of the room was composed of the same strange substance as the walls, and when struck gave out a sound which Uncle Prudent was unable to class in the list of known sounds. Another strange fact —this floor sounded hollow, as if it was not resting on the soil of the clearing, and the inexplicable whir sounded as strong underneath as it did above and around them. These things were certainly not reassuring.

"Uncle Prudent!" said Phil Evans.

"Phil Evans!"

"Do you think that our prison has been moved?"

"By no means."

"Nevertheless, for a little while after our incarceration in this cell I was able to detect the fresh odor of plants and the resinous perfume of the trees in the park. Now, when I inhale the air it seems to me that all these odors have disappeared."

"Indeed!"

"How do you explain this fact?"

"We can not explain it at all, Phil Evans, unless by supposing that our prison has changed place, and I repeat that if such had been the case we would have felt the movement."

Frycollin uttered a long groan, which would have been taken for his last breath if he had not followed it with several more.

"I hope that this Robur will soon put an end to our conjectures by having us brought before him," said Phil Evans.

"I hope so too," returned Uncle Prudent, "and I will tell him—"

"What?"

"That after having commenced like a fool he has finished like a knave."

At this moment Phil Evans noticed that day was beginning to break. A light, still vague, was beginning to struggle through the narrow window cut in the wall opposite the door.

It must be about four in the morning, since that is the hour during the month of June when the horizon of Philadelphia is whitened by the first rays of dawn.

Uncle Prudent sounded the repeater of his watch—a *chef d'œuvre* from the factory of his colleague—and the little bell struck quarter to three.

"Strange," said Phil Evans. "At quarter to three it is still night."

"My watch must be a little slow," replied Uncle Prudent.

"A watch of the Walton Watch Company? Never!" cried the secretary.

But be this as it may, day was certainly breaking, and the obscurity of the room was lightening.

"Now that it is nearly day outside, we might be able to gain some clew to our situation through the window there," said Phil Evans.

"We can try," said Uncle Prudent, and turning to Frycollin: "Come, Fry, get up."

The negro raised himself.

"Put your back against that wall," continued Uncle Prudent, "and you, Phil Evans, mount on his shoulder and see if you can throw any light on this mystery."

"Willingly," replied Phil Evans, and the next moment he had his feet on Frycollin's shoulders and his eyes on a level with the window. The window was closed with a single pane of glass, which, while not very thick, was not very clear, and obstructed the view of the secretary, whose eyesight at any time was not too good.

"Well, break the glass," said Uncle Prudent, "and perhaps you can see better."

Phil Evans struck the window a violent blow with his bowie-knife. The glass gave a ringing sound, but did not break. A second blow, more violent than the first. Same result.

"Good!" cried Phil Evans. "Unbreakable glass."

In fact, the pane must have been composed of glass tempered by the process of the inventor, Siemens, since, in spite of repeated blows, it remained intact.

However, it had now become light enough outside to see

dimly through the glass, but the range of sight was limited
by the small size of the narrow window.

" What do you see?" asked Uncle Prudent.

" Nothing."

" What? Not a clump of trees?"

" No."

" Not even the tops of the trees?"

" Not a branch."

" Are we not in the clearing?"

" Neither in the clearing, nor in the park."

" Can you not see at least the roofs of the houses or the
tops of monuments?" said Uncle Prudent, whose disappointment and fury were increasing.

" Neither roofs nor monuments."

" What! Not even a flag-staff or a church, or even a
factory chimney?"

" Nothing but space."

At this moment the door opened. A man appeared on
the threshold. It was Robur.

" Honorable balloonists," said he in a grave voice, " you
are now free to go and come—"

" Free!" cried Uncle Prudent.

" Yes—within the limits of the ' Albatross.' "

Uncle Prudent and Phil Evans precipitated themselves
out of the cell.

And where were they?

Three thousand feet beneath them they saw the surface
of a country which they tried in vain to recognize.

CHAPTER VI.

A CHAPTER WHICH BOTH SCIENTISTS AND DUNCES HAD BETTER OMIT.

" WHEN will man cease to grovel on the earth and dwell in the peaceful and azure heavens?"

This question of Camille Flammarion is easily answered. It will be the age in which mechanical progress has solved the problem of flying. And for some years past a practical utilization of electricity has been conducting us rapidly to a solution of this problem.

In 1783, before the Montgolfier Brothers and the physician Charles had constructed their first balloons, a few adventurous minds were dreaming of the conquest of space with the aid of flying machines.

The first inventors had not attempted to realize aerial locomotion with structures lighter than air, the balloon, for instance, but their endeavors were directed toward heavy cumbersome flying machines built in imitation of birds. It was this principle that inspired that fool Icarus, son of Dædalus, whose wings of wax melted on approaching the sun.

But without going back to mythological ages, without speaking of Archytas, of Tarente, we find already in the works of Dante de Perouse, of Leonardi de Vinci, and of Guidotti, the germs from which the art of flying will develop.

Some centuries after, the inventors increased in number

In 1742 Marquis de Bacqueville manufactured a system
of wings, tried them over the banks of the Seine, and fell
and broke his arm.   In 1768 Paucton conceived the idea
of a machine with two propellers, one suspensive, the other
propulsive.

In 1784 Launoy and Bienvenu constructed a machine the
motive power of which was formed of springs which drove
a propeller.

Trials at flight were made in 1808 by the Austrian,
Jacques Degen, and from 1811 to 1840 essays and inven-
tions were advanced by Berblinger, Vignal, Sarti, Dubochet,
Cagniard and Latour.

In 1842 we find the Englishman, Henson, with his system of inclined planes and steam propellers.   In 1852
Letur's experience with his dirigible parachute cost him
his life.   From 1854 to 1863 appeared Joseph Pline,
Breant, Carlingford, Du Temple, Bright, Smythies, and
Edison, some with wings, others with screws, imagining,
creating, and perfecting machines and preparing the road
for the time when some inventor shall evolve the perfect
work.

The different forms of the attempts made by the above
inventors may be summed up into three classes:

1. Helicopters—Machines propelled by screws on vertical
   axles.
2. Orthopters, reproducing the natural flight of birds.
3. Aeroplanes, propelled by screws on horizontal axles-

Each of these systems had, and even yet possesses,
stanch partisans unwilling to concede a point to the sup-

porters of different systems. That the orthopter or mechanical bird presents certain advantages no one will doubt. But then, although it is wise to imitate nature, it is not absolutely necessary to do so servilely. Locomotives have not been copied from hares, and instead of legs possess wheels. Steamships are not exact models of fishes, and do not even boast a single fin, and yet they can hardly 'oe classed as failures. Besides, is it possible to mechanically imitate the complex movements of the flight of a bird? Dr. Morey has shown that when a bird raises a wing the feathers open to permit the passage of air, a movement which would be difficult to imitate with an artificial machine.

Robur rejected the first two of these systems and accepted the latter as the least complicated and most effective method of flight, that is, the aeroplane, and combined it with the orthopter this far: A screw necessarily revolves in the same direction with its axis. If the axis is vertical the screw displaces air vertically. If the axis is horizontal the screw displaces air horizontally. The flying machine invented by Robur was based on these two simple facts. To exactly describe this machine it will be necessary to divide it into three parts—the platform, the engines of suspension and propulsion, and the machinery. The platform, a large deck, ninety feet long, twenty-three feet wide, with a beak-shaped bow below, a strongly built hull, which contained the engines which supplied the motive power, the store-room, implements and the water tanks. Light upright posts supported a hand-rail, which extended around the entire structure. The tops of three turrets were raised above the deck. In the central turret was the machine which drove the suspensive engines. In the one nearest the bow was the machinery of the front propeller, and in the turret at the stern was placed the machinery of the rear propeller. The kitchen, office, and pantry were situated near the turret at the bow, and the dining-room, sleeping cabins and other apartments were placed at the stern. The turrets and rooms were lighted through port-holes closed with tempered glass, the resisting power of which was ten times greater than ordinary glass. Suspensory and propelling engines—Above the platform thirty-seven axles were raised, fifteen on each side and seven in the middle of the deck. Each of these axles supported two screws of short diameter and channel, but which were capable of revolving with prodigious speed, and each of which revolved independently of the others and in opposite direction. In the front and rear were two propulsory screws with larger branches than the suspensory screws, but which were capable of revolving with the same speed.

Machinery—Robur obtained the power necessary to propel his machine, neither from steam, compressed air, nor explosive mixtures, but was assisted by an agent which one day will be the acknowledged life of the industrial world, electricity. The composition of the batteries, the nature of the positive and negative poles, is a secret which has been carefully guarded by Robur, and they supplied a greater force, and imparted a swifter motion to the axles than could have been obtained by the use of any heretofore invented electric battery.

The stability of the whole structure was assured by a careful compliance with the laws of gravity, and there was no danger of overturning.

There still remains to be explained the nature of the material that had been employed by Robur in the construction of his air ship—a name which exactly describes "Albatross." What was the strange substance which had resisted Phil Evans's bowie-knife, and which Uncle Prudent was unable to recognize?

Paper.

During the past few years this industry has been rapidly developing. Unsized paper, impregnated with dextrine and starch and submitted to hydraulic pressure, is transformed into a substance as hard as steel. It is possible to manufacture from this substance rails and even car-wheels stronger than metal wheels, and at the same time lighter, and it was this solidity and lightness that Robur had utilized in the construction of his aerial locomotive. Hull, deck, turrets, cabins, all were made of paper, which, under pressure, had become as strong as metal and as incombustible.

For the different parts of the engines, axles and screws, a strong and flexible material was also supplied by paper. Insoluble in gas or liquids, and resisting acids and other corrosive fluids—without speaking of its insulating properties—this paper proved very useful in the construction of the electric machinery of the "Albatross."

The captain, Robur; his foreman George Kerns, an engineer, two assistants, two steersmen, and a chief cook, in all eight men, comprised the *personnel* of the "Alba-

tross," and formed a crew which were amply sufficient for
the execution of all the maneuvers required in aerial locomotion.

Rifles, pistols, and, smile if you will, fishing-tackle, electric lamps, instruments of observation, compasses and sex-
tants for laying out the route, thermometers, different
forms of barometers, some for calculating the height,
others for indicating atmospheric pressure, a storm glass for
the prevision of tempests, a small library, a breech-load-
ing cannon mounted on a pivot in the center of the deck,
stores of powder, balls, cartridges and dynamite, a pantry
filled with cooking-utensils, kitchen heated by a current
from the batteries, a store-room filled with a stock of conserves, canned meats and vegetables ranged *ad hoc* with
casks of brandy, whisky and gin—these constituted all the
stores and provisions of the air-ship, excepting the famous
trumpet.

In addition there was a light, insubmersible rubber boat,
capable of carrying eight men on the surface of a river,
lake or even a calm sea. So much for safety on water, but
had not Robur at least provided himself with parachutes
to be used in case of accidents? No. He did not believe
in accidents. The axles of the screws each revolved independently of the others, and the stoppage of one would
not interfere with the movement of another, and the working of one fifth of the number of the screws was sufficient
to maintain the " Albatross " in its natural element.

" And with this vessel," as Robur the Conqueror had
occasion to say to his new guests, " with this vessel I am
master of a world larger than all Europe, Asia, Africa,

America, and Australia combined, an aerial world which a
future age will see inhabited by a million descendants of
Icarus.''

———

CHAPTER VII.

UNCLE PRUDENT AND PHIL EVANS STILL REFUSE TO BE CONVINCED.

THE president of the Weldon Club was stupefied, his
companion astounded, but both endeavored to conceal a
fright that, under the circumstances, was pardonable. The
valet Frycollin, however, made no attempt to disguise his
feelings and poured out lamentable cries of terror at seeing
himself borne through space at a frightful rate of speed.

The suspensory screws were at this time revolving over
their heads with a rapidity that seemed to them prodigious,
but which would have been tripled had Robur desired to
ascend still higher.   The two propellers were turning
slowly, and imparted to the vessel a speed of only thirty
miles an hour.   Leaning over the rail of the deck, the passengers of the "Albatross" saw thousands of feet below
them the surface of an undulating country dotted with several small ponds.   They could even at intervals catch a
glitter as the oblique rays of the sun gleamed across the
waters below, and could trace the outline of a long and
sinuous liquid belt which like a little brook wound in and
out between the hills.   This brook was a river, and one of
the most important of the country.   On the left bank
started a chain of mountains, the continuation of which was
lost in the distance.

" And now where are we?" demanded Uncle Prudent,
his voice trembling with rage.

" That question must remain for the present unanswered," replied Robur.

" And where are we going?" asked Phil Evans.

" Across space."

" And this thing will end—"

" When I am ready."

" Perhaps we will make a tour of the world?" inquired
Phil Evans, ironically.

" We shall do more than that," responded Robur.

" And if this voyage does not suit us?" said Uncle
Prudent.

" You will find it necessary to make it suit you."

This is but a foretaste of the relations which were established between the master of the " Albatross " and his
guests, not to say prisoners. But Robur evidently wished
to give them time to recover from their astonishment and
to admire the marvelous machine which bore them through
the air, and he walked to the other end of the deck, leaving the passengers at liberty to examine the mechanism
and working of the air-ship or to view the country which
they passed over.

" Uncle Prudent," said Phil Evans, " unless I am mistaken we are over the central portion of Canada. That
river which flows in the south-west is the St. Lawrence, and
the city we are now leaving in our rear must be Quebec."

It was in truth the old city of Champlain, whose roofs of
tin glittered in the sun like mirrors. The " Albatross "
was consequently about forty-six degrees north, which ex-

plained the early break of day, and the prolongation of the dawn.

"Yes," continued Phil Evans, "it is Quebec, for on that hill to the right is the citadel of the Gibraltar of North America. There are the English and French cathedrals. That building, from the dome of which floats a British flag, is the custom-house."

Phil Evans had hardly finished speaking before the capital of Canada began to fade away in the distance. The air-ship entered into a zone of clouds which gradually shut out the view.

Robur, seeing that the president and secretary were now devoting their attention to the working of the "Albatross," approached them and said:

"Well, gentlemen, do you believe now in the possibility of aerial locomotion in machines heavier than air?"

It was useless to argue against the proofs they had before them. Nevertheless, Uncle Prudent and Phil Evans remained silent.

"You seem to hesitate," said Robur. "But I forgot. Hunger probably prevents you from answering my question. Although I have undertaken the task of transporting you through the air I shall not attempt to feed you with ethereal substance. Your first breakfast awaits your convenience."

As the pangs of hunger had commenced to stir within both Uncle Prudent and Phil Evans, they immediately decided that it was not a time for ceremony. A meal or two made no pledges, and they resolved that when Robur replaced them on the earth they would not allow a paltry breakfast to hamper their liberty of action in dealing with this audacious wretch.

They were conducted to the rear turret into a little dining-room. There they found a table, correctly set, from which they were to eat during the voyage. A dainty and inviting repast was placed before them, and in a few minutes they felt as much at home as if they were sitting at their favorite table in their beloved Continental Hotel.

Frycollin had not been forgotten and had been served with food of more substantial and solid qualities, but strange to say, the food remained untouched. His teeth chattered with fear and refused to serve him.

"Suppose the machinery breaks," groaned the unhappy negro.

"Well, suppose it does, Frycollin. What then? A fall of 4,500 feet would only grind you to powder, and you would not even feel it."

An hour later, Uncle Prudent and Phil Evans reappeared on the deck. Robur was nowhere to be seen. At the stern, the steersman in his glass cage, his eyes fixed on the compass, was imperturbably following the route given him by Robur. The rest of the crew were all at breakfast, excepting an assistant engineer, who was walking from one turret to the other, carefully watching the machinery.

The "Albatross" was now flying at a height of about 4,000 feet above the earth and in a short time emerged from the mass of clouds in which it had been immersed for over an hour and the passengers could again obtain a view of the country beneath.

"I can hardly believe all this," said Phil Evans.

"Do not try to believe it," replied Uncle Prudent, "we are dreaming."

They crossed to the bow and directed their gaze toward the western horizon.

"Ah, another city!" exclaimed the secretary.

"Can you recognize it?"

"Yes. I think it is Montreal."

"Montreal? But it has not been two hours since we left Quebec."

"Which proves that this machine can travel at least seventy-five miles an hour."

This was really the rate of speed with which the air-ship was now flying, and the reason the passengers had not felt it was that they were traveling with the wind. In a calm atmosphere they would have been seriously inconvenienced, and against a contrary wind they would have been unable to appear on deck.

Phil Evans had not been deceived. Below the "Albatross" was the city of Montreal, easily recognized by the Victoria Bridge, a tubular span thrown across the St. Lawrence River like the railway viaduct over the Venetian lagoons. They also distinguished the city by the large streets, the size of the houses and by the cathedral modeled after the St. Peter at Rome. It was fortunate that Phil Evans was familiar with the principal cities of Canada, as he was enabled to recognize some of them without questioning Robur.

An hour and a half after leaving Montreal they passed over Ottawa, and could see the falls falling like a streak

3

of silver into an immense boiler, which bubbled and
foamed like a monster caldron.

"There is the Parliament House," said Phil Evans,
pointing to a sort of Nuremburg toy, which was perched
on the side of a hill.   This toy, with its diversified style of
architecture, resembled the Houses of Parliament of London, the Montreal Cathedral, and the Saint Peter of
Rome.

About two hours later Robur reappeared, accompanied
by his foreman, George Kerns.   He passed by Uncle Prudent and Phil Evans, looked at a gauge that was affixed to
the central turret, and gave an order to the two assistants
in the turret.   At a sign, the steersman altered the course
of the " Albatross " to the south-west.   Uncle Prudent and
Phil Evans observed that a highly increased speed had
been imparted to the propellers.   The air-ship was now
flying at a speed which surpassed that ever attained by any
engine of terrestrial locomotion.   Steamboats travel about
22 knots, or 25 miles an hour; the locomotives of France
and England have reached 60 miles an hour; ice-boats,
used on the frozen surface of rivers in the United States,
67 miles an hour; a locomotive manufactured at Paterson,
N. J., has covered 80 miles an hour over the Lake Erie
road, and another engine, used on a Pennsylvania road,
has reached the marvelous speed of 84 miles an hour.
Compare these figures with the following, and you will see
that the fastest locomotive would follow like a snail in the
track of the " Albatross. "   The maximum power produced
by the propellers of the " Albatross " produced a speed
of 125 miles an hour, or about 183 feet a second.   This is

the speed of the cyclone, which tears along at about 176 feet a second. It is the rate at which the carrier-pigeon flies, and is only exceeded by the flight of the common swallow, 207 feet a second, and by that of the martin or swift, 260 feet a second.

In a word, the "Albatross," as Robur had asserted at the stormy meeting of the Weldon Club, could, by exerting all the power of its screws, make a tour of the world in two hundred hours, or about eight days.

It was this speed that had enabled Robur to mystify the inhabitants of the lower world by appearing with the "Albatross" over Asia and America in the same week. The flaring notes of the famous trumpet were sounded by the foreman, George Kerns. The ensign which covered the "Albatross" was the flag of Robur the Conqueror—a golden sun on a black ground, surrounded with stars.

Until now Robur had taken precautions to take his soaring flights unobserved and had only traveled by night, depending on the use of his electric light, and during the day retiring behind masses of clouds. Now he seemed no longer desirous of keeping his conquest a secret, and had even alighted in the very heart of civilization and appeared in person in the drawing-room of the Weldon Club. We know the nature of his reception by the meeting, but have yet to learn what method of retaliation he would adopt with the president and secretary of the said club. Robur approached the two colleagues. They were striving to conceal their amazement at what they saw around them, and were prepared to dispute and resist their captor to the end. Robur paid no attention to their perverse and antag-

onistic attitude, and continued the conversation that had
been interrupted two hours previous.

"Gentlemen, you are undoubtedly asking yourselves
whether this machine, so admirably fitted for aerial locomotion, is capable of attaining a higher rate of speed. It
would not be worthy of conquering space if it was unable
to consume it. I have told you that to me the air is a
solid body, and it is. I have shown you that to successfully battle with the wind one has only to be stronger than
the wind, and I am stronger. I ask the assistance of
neither sails, oars, wheels nor rails, and have but one element—air. The air surrounds the 'Albatross' precisely
the same as water surrounds a submarine boat, and my
propellers drive through the air as the screw of a steamer
cuts the water. This is my method of solving the problem
of flying, and you must admit that it is certainly not a
failure, and this is why I so confidently asserted that in the
science of ballooning there is no future."

Uncle Prudent and Phil Evans remained silent, and appeared not to have heard these words, but Robur was not
for an instant disconcerted. He contented himself with
a half smile and continued:

"Perhaps you are asking whether to this power of
horizontal speed the 'Albatross' can add an equal power of
vertical speed; in a word, whether the 'Albatross' can
compete with a balloon in a rapid ascent to the highest
zones of the air. Well, I would not advise you to back
the 'Go-ahead' against the 'Albatross' in such a con-
test."

The two colleagues shrugged their shoulders, as if they

would prefer to see these things attempted before believing them possible.

Robur turned toward the turret, and made a motion with his hand. The propulsive screws stopped instantly, the "Albatross" gradually slowed up, and in a minute hung almost motionless. At a second gesture from Robur the suspensive screws began to turn with incredible rapidity, giving a strange whir. The machine shot up like a rocket, and as the rarefaction of the air increased, the whir decreased in proportion.

"Master, master, save me!" cried Frycollin, who was writhing in terror on the deck. A disdainful smile was Robur's only response to this appeal. In a few minutes the barometer showed that a height of thirteen thousand feet had been reached, and the "Albatross" descended again.

The supply of oxygen decreases with the density of the air, and this fact occasions the greatest of the dangers of aerial navigation, and Robur did not desire to expose his guests to this danger. The "Albatross" returned to the height which Robur usually preferred, and bore rapidly to the south-west.

"Now, gentlemen, I believe I have answered everything," said the inventor, and he crossed to the other end of the deck, where he remained absorbed in reflection. When he raised his head again the president and secretary of the Weldon Club stood before him.

"Captain Robur," said Uncle Prudent, vainly struggling to restrain his rage, "we have asked you nothing as yet, and did not solicit your views on aerial navigation.

But I am about to ask you a question to which I expect a straight reply."

" Proceed. "

" By what right did you attack us in Fairmount Park? By what right did you confine us in that cell? By what right have you carried us, against our will, on board of this flying machine?"

" And by what right, my balloonist friends, did you insult, mock and threaten me in your club-house? By what right did you attempt personal violence on a man whose only crime was that he held opinions that differed from yours?"

" You answer our question by asking another," said Phil Evans, " and we repeat, by what right?"

" Do you wish to know."

" That *was* our object in asking."

" Well, then, by the right of the strongest.'

" You are impudent."

" Possibly, but truthful."

" And for how long," demanded Uncle Prudent, who was now white with rage, " do you contemplate exercising this pretended right?"

" What, gentlemen, you ask such a question when you have only to lower your eyes to be afforded a sight without equal in the world."

They were crossing the country which has been so poetically described by Fenimore Cooper. Below, like a mirror, stretched out the vast expanse of Lake Ontario. Passing over the lake, they followed the course of the river, which a little later precipitates itself over the famous cataracts. A majestic roar like the blast of the tempest was carried up to them, and the atmosphere freshened as if a fog had closed around them. The river wound its way like a crystal stream through a thousand rainbows, which seemed to arch themselves over it, and, reaching the falls, trembled, sparkled and took the final plunge, shaking the earth for miles around.

It was a sublime sight. A foot-bridge hung like a thread between the two banks of the river, and about three miles below the falls swung a suspension bridge, over which a train was crossing from the Canadian to the American side.

"The cataracts of Niagara!" cried Phil Evans, while Uncle Prudent exerted all his efforts to conceal his admiration at the panorama below them.

A minute later the " Albatross " had cleared the river which separates the United States from the Canadian colonies and started like a rocket across the vast territory of North America.

CHAPTER VIII.

ROBUR PRACTICALLY RESPONDS TO UNCLE PRUDENT'S QUESTION.

UNCLE PRUDENT and Phil Evans were assigned to one of the cabins in the stern of the " Albatross," and found there two excellent beds, changes of linen, traveling garments, and everything required to make them comfortable. If they did not sleep very soundly it was not the fault of their surroundings, but of the inquietude with which they

themselves were filled. On what strange adventure had
they started, what experience awaited them, how would the
affair terminate and, most important of all, why had Robur captured them? These were the questions they asked
themselves, and to which they sought in vain for answers.

As for Frycollin, he had been installed in a cabin near
to the cook of the " Albatross." The neighborhood did
not altogether displease him, as he liked to mingle with
the great men of the world, and to him a cook was a god.
But if he found sleep at all that night it was only to dream
of successive falls and of flights across space that turned
his slumber into an abominable nightmare. Notwithstanding the fears of the passengers, nothing could have
been more peaceful or calm than that midnight journey
through the air. Not a sound around them save the whir
of the screws. Then, at intervals they could catch a faint
whistle, which was carried up to them from some terrestrial locomotive; or, as the " Albatross " approached
nearer to the earth, the howls of wild animals could be
faintly heard. Singular instinct. These terrestrial animals scented the flying machine passing above them and
howled in fright at the sight of the strange bird. The
morning of the 14th of June, at five o'clock, Uncle
Prudent and Phil Evans appeared on the deck of the " Albatross." Nothing had changed since the preceding
night; a sentinel on guard at the bow, and the steersman
in his cage at the stern.

Why was the sentinel there? Was there any danger of
a collision with some other aerial machine? Evidently
Robur had not as yet found any imitators, and the chances

for meeting a balloonist at that altitude were infinitely small. And if such a meeting had occurred it was all up with the balloonist, the pot of iron and the pot of clay. The "Albatross" had therefore nothing to fear from a collision of this kind, but there was a real danger which it was necessary to carefully guard against. If the "Albatross" instead of passing or clearing a mountain were to collide with it the machine would upset like a vessel. A ship is compelled to guard against the rocks of the seas, and the "Albatross" took the same precautions against the rocks of the air.

Uncle Prudent and Phil Evans again turned their attention toward the country beneath them, and they discovered in the distance a vast lake, to the southern extremity of which they were now heading. They concluded that during the night they must have left Lake Erie in their rear, and as their course had been in a westerly direction, were now reaching the lower end of Lake Michigan.

"There is not a doubt of it," said Phil Evans. "That group of house-tops in the horizon there is Chicago."

He had not been deceived. It was indeed that city from which seventeen lines of railroads radiate, the Queen of the West, the vast reservoir into which flow the products of Illinois, Wisconsin, Iowa, Missouri and of the states which form the western part of the Union. Uncle Prudent, armed with an excellent marine glass which he had found in the cabin, could easily distinguish the principal edifices of the city. His colleague named the different structures, churches, public buildings, grain elevators, and pointed out the immense Sherman House, which from its

elevation resembled an enormous die, with windows marking the points in the side.

"Since this is Chicago," said Uncle Prudent, "we are
evidently going further west than we desire."

In fact the "Albatross" was leaving the Illinois city
behind it at every turn of the propellers.

But had Uncle Prudent desired to request Robur to
change his course to the east he could not have done so at
that moment, for the inventor was either occupied with
some work or was still sleeping, as he had not yet appeared
from his cabin. The two colleagues breakfasted without
meeting him.

The rate of speed at which they traveled during the
night was still continued undiminished. They were going
with the wind, which came from the east; and the thermometer standing at seventy degrees, the temperature was
very comfortable, and while waiting for the appearance of
Robur the two colleagues devoted their time to an examination of the structure and mechanism of the air-ship, and
to the working of the screws which were revolving with
such rapidity that the light glancing from their branches
formed itself into a semi-diaphanous disk.

The northern portion of the state of Illinois had been
crossed in less than three hours. The "Albatross" passed
over the "Father of Waters," the Mississippi, the double-
docked steamboats on whose surface appearing to the voy-
agers above about as large as canoes. Then the "Albatross" started across Iowa, after passing Iowa City about
eleven o'clock in the morning.

Several chains of mountains and bluffs wound through

this country obliquely from the south to the north-west, but their altitude did not necessitate any alteration in the height of the air-ship's course. These mountains gradually decreased in height until they were replaced by the large plains which stretch over the greater part of Iowa and Nebraska—immense prairies which extended to the base of the Rocky Mountains. Here and there, on the banks of the numerous tributary streams of the Missouri River, cities and villages could be seen, but which decreased in size and number as the "Albatross" rapidly advanced into the west.

Nothing of particular importance transpired during the day, and Uncle Prudent and Phil Evans were left to themselves.

Even Frycollin remained quiet, stretched out on the deck, his eyes closed, striving to shut out the frightful view around him. Frycollin's fear was not due as much to vertigo as one would imagine, for he would not have experienced the same fright from the top of a lofty steeple or monument. Looking over the car of a balloon or from the platform of an air-ship it is not the depths immediately beneath us that fill us with dread; it is the horizon which encircles us.

At two o'clock the "Albatross" passes over Omaha, on the frontiers of Nebraska—the central point of the numerous lines of railroad which cross the country between New York and San Francisco.

For a moment they could see the yellow waters of the Missouri, and then the brick and wooden houses of the city passed beneath them. While they were observing these

things the inhabitants of Omaha were exciting themselves
at the sight of the "Albatross." They were probably as
astonished at seeing it cut through the air as the president
and secretary of the Weldon Club were at being on board
of the strange machine. At all events, it furnished the
newspapers of the country with a clew to the extraordinary
phenomenon which had baffled them and the entire world
for a few months back. An hour later the "Albatross"
had left Omaha far in the rear and, steering to the west,
crossed the Platte River, and followed the line of the
Pacific Railway across the prairie. This course apparently
did not please Uncle Prudent and Phil Evans.

"Can this man be serious in his project of carrying us
to the other side of the world?" asked one.

"He does not dare to do it," replied the other. "Ah!
Robur, take care. I am not a man to be trifled with."

"Nor I!" joined Phil Evans. "But take my advice,
Uncle Prudent, and be calm and save your rage for the
moment when you can use it to advantage."

About five o'clock, after having crossed the Black
Hills, covered with fir and cedar trees, the "Albatross" flew over the territory which has justly been named
the Bad Lands of Nebraska—a chaos of ocher-colored hills,
of fragments of mountains which were scattered across the
country in uneven chains. From a distance these hills
and mountains took the most fantastic forms and seemed
endowed with life.

Not a sign of vegetation for miles around, and the country looked like an immense cemetery where the bones of a
thousand animals lay whitening in the sun. By night they

had passed the basin of the Platte River, and continued on their westerly course. During the night the calm of the air around them was broken neither by the shrill shriek of locomotives nor the piercing whistle of steamboats, but as the "Albatross" dipped nearer the earth the sentinel could hear a long rolling sound. This was the bellowing of the buffalo herds who were crossing the prairie in search of water and pasturage. At intervals this noise would be mingled with the howl of a wolf or coyote, or the cry of a wild cat. Then as the dawn approached everything became still.

The next morning, the 15th of June, Phil Evans left his cabin at about five o'clock, thinking he might probably meet Robur, but he was unable to see the captain either on the deck or in the dining-room. He resolved to discover, at all events, why Robur had not appeared during the day previous, and he addressed himself to the foreman, George Kerns. George Kerns was of English origin, about forty-five years of age, with a large and characteristic head surmounting a powerfully built body. A man of a practical turn of mind and of a mechanical knowledge that rendered him invaluable to his captain.

"Shall we see Captain Robur to-day?" inquired Phil Evans.

"I do not know."

"Has he gone out?" asked the secretary, sarcastically.

"Perhaps."

"When will he return?"

"When it suits him to do so."

And George Kerns entered his cabin.

This interview was not very reassuring to the secretary, and a glance at the compass showed that the course of the "Albatross" was due north-west, which made him still more uncomfortable.

There was a striking contrast between the arid territory of the "Bad Lands," which they had left behind them during the night, and the country which was now unfolding before them. Omaha was now many miles in their rear, and they found themselves over a country which Phil Evans was unable to recognize, for the simple reason that he had never visited it. Two forts, built for protection against the Indians, crowned the bluffs in geometrical lines, formed by the palisades and walls around them; and the rising sun traced the outlines, still faint, of a chain of mountains in the west.

They were the Rocky Mountains. All at once Uncle Prudent and Phil Evans shivered with cold. This lowering of the temperature was not due to a change of the weather, as the sun was still shining brightly.

"The 'Albatross' must be ascending," said Phil Evans. Such was the case. The barometer on the door of the central turret indicated that they were now at an elevation of about ten thousand feet, and were still rising and crossing the snow-capped mountains beneath them.

Uncle Prudent and his companion were endeavoring to recognize the country, but the flights north and south made by the "Albatross" during the night had disturbed their reckoning. However, after a little discussion, they concluded that the country below them, circled by a chain of mountains, was that territory which by an act of Congress, in March, 1872, had been declared the National Park of the United States. It was, indeed, that curious region which well merits the name of park—a park which for hills had mountains; for ponds, lakes; for brooks, rivers; and for fountains, geysers of wonderful power.

In a few minutes the "Albatross" glided above the Yellowstone River, and, with Mount Stevenson on the right, passed over Yellowstone Lake. Here was an opportunity for the chief cook to lay in a supply of trout, the only fish that exists in the waters of the Yellowstone, but the height of the "Albatross" was too great for scientific fly fishing and the cook scorned to capture a trout in any other manner. The lake was cleared in about half an hour and a little later they reached the geysers, which rival those of Iceland. From their position on the deck Uncle Prudent and Phil Evans could see the liquid column darting up toward them as if striving to reach the air-ship.

They could see the "Fan" spreading out its magnificent jets, "Old Faithful" crowded with rainbows and the "Giant" spurting out a vertical torrent, twenty feet in circumference, to a height of over two hundred feet. Robur was familiar with all the wonders of this incomparable spectacle, for he did not appear on deck. Was it only to please his guests that he had directed the "Albatross" over the National Park? If this had been his object, he evidently did not wish to seek their thanks. He had not even shown himself during the flight over the Rocky Mountains at seven o'clock that morning.

By increasing the speed of the suspensory propellers the "Albatross" could easily have cleared the highest peak in

the chain of mountains, but this maneuver had not been
necessary. There were passes and canyons in the mountains formed like roofless tunnels, and it was through one
of these canyons that the " Albatross " passed.

The speed was moderated, and the steersman, with a
sure hand, aided by the extreme sensibility of the steering
machinery, guided the air-ship as gently and as truly as a
racing shell. The two enemies of the " heavier than air "
were unable to repress their admiration at this new triumph of the marvelous machine they were standing on.

In less than three hours the great chain was crossed, and
the " Albatross " resumed its original speed, taking its
course to the south-west in such a manner as to cut
obliquely across Utah Territory, and gradually lowered
toward the earth. It had descended some hundred yards
when the sound of a shrill whistle attracted the attention
of Uncle Prudent and Phil Evans.

It was a train on the Pacific Railway on its way to Salt
Lake City.

At the same time, in obedience to a secret order from
Robur, the " Albatross " drew nearer still to the earth,
and followed the train so closely that the air-ship was surrounded with the smoke from the engine. The machine was
instantly perceived. The car windows were crowded with
heads, and the platforms were thronged with passengers,
some even climbing to the tops of the cars to obtain a better view of the flying machine. Cheers and hurrahs came
through space to the air-ship, but even they failed to bring
Robur on deck.

The " Albatross " descended still lower, moderating the

action of the suspensory screws and, slowing up in speed in order to keep pace with the train, commenced a series of aerial maneuvers around the bewildered travelers below. It darted swiftly to the right and left, circled around the train like a gigantic bird of prey, took long flights to the rear, and then turning back overtook the locomotive with a single bound. Then the black flag with the golden sun was hoisted and the engineer below responded by waving the thirty-seven-starred flag of the American Union. In vain did the two prisoners endeavor to profit by the occasion to make known their identity. In vain the president of the Weldon Club shouted in a loud voice:

"I am Uncle Prudent, of Philadelphia."

And the secretary:

"I am Phil Evans, his colleague."

Their cries were lost in the thousand hurrahs with which the travelers saluted their passengers. In the meantime three or four of the crew of the air-ship had appeared on deck. One of them—after the fashion of sailors passing a slower vessel than their own—threw a rope out to the train, an ironical method of offering a tow.

The "Albatross" continued its usual speed, and in a short time the train was out of sight in the rear.

An hour after noon a large disk appeared in the distance, reflecting the rays of the sun like a mirror.

"It must be the Mormon capital, Salt Lake City," said Uncle Prudent. It was, in fact, the Mormon city, and the disk was the round roof of the Tabernacle in which ten thousand saints could move at ease, and the dome of which scattered the rays of the sun in all directions like a convex

mirror. The city faded away like a shadow, and the
"Albatross" bore to the south-west with increased
rapidity, and was in a few hours taking its flight over the
silver-producing sections of Nevada, which are only separated by the Sierra Nevada Mountains from the auriferous
regions of California.

"If this speed continues we shall see San Francisco before night," said Phil Evans.

"And after that?" asked Uncle Prudent.

It was exactly six o'clock in the evening as the "Albatross" cleared the last peak of the Sierra Nevadas, and
there only needed to be covered one hundred and ninety-
eight miles to reach Sacramento, the capital of California.

The speed at which the "Albatross" was now flying was
so great that at ten minutes to eight the dome of the Sacramento court-house was sighted in the western horizon.
A few minutes later Robur appeared on deck. The two
colleagues advanced toward him.

"Captain Robur," said Uncle Prudent, "we are now
at the western shore of America. It is time to finish your
jest—"

"I never jest," replied Robur. He gave an order to
one of the crew, and the "Albatross" descended rapidly
toward the earth and at the same time the speed was increased to such a degree that the two prisoners were forced
to take refuge in the turret.

"A moment more and I should have strangled him,"
said Uncle Prudent.

"We are nearing the earth and may find an opportunity
to escape, and escape we will," replied Phil Evans.

"Yes, at any cost."

A prolonged murmur reached their ears.

It was the grinding of the sea breaking on the rocks of the coast.

It was the Pacific Ocean.

CHAPTER IX.

THE "ALBATROSS" TERMINATES A LONG FLIGHT WITH A PRODIGIOUS LEAP.

UNCLE PRUDENT and Phil Evans had firmly resolved to escape. If the crew of the air-ship had not comprised eight particularly vigorous men perhaps they would have attempted to fight for their liberty. An audacious stroke might render them masters of the machine, and they could then descend to some point in the United States.

But, with only two against eight—Frycollin was only counted as a negative quantity—it was not to be dreamed of. Since force was not to be employed it was necessary to resort to strategy.

This fact Phil Evans endeavored to impress upon his irascible colleague, who, he feared, would attempt some premature violence that would aggravate the situation. At all events, the time for flight had not yet arrived. The air-ship was shooting at full speed over the North Pacific Ocean. The morning of the 16th of June not a trace of land could be seen around them. Captain Robur, either through habit or attention, had remained in his turret during a larger part of the time.

This morning as he appeared he contented himself with saluting his two guests as he passed them on his way to the stern of the air-ship. His eyes, reddened by loss of sleep, with a stupefied air, his legs trembling, Frycollin was just venturing out of his cabin, walking like a man balancing himself on a tight-rope. His first care was to see if the suspensory screw, which was working with reassuring regularity, was all right.

This done, the negro, trembling in every limb, started for the side of the "Albatross" and seized the hand-rail with both hands to steady himself. Evidently he wished to get a view of the country over which the "Albatross" was flying at a height of two thousand feet.

He also wished to convince his master by looking over the side that he was very audacious and brave. He walked backward until he reached the bulwarks, which he felt all over to get the strongest portion; then he slowly turned around and bent his head over the side.

It is useless to remark that during the execution of these movements his eyes were closed.

At last he opened them.

With a wild shriek he sprung back, his head buried between his hands.

Below him he had seen the immense ocean.

"The sea! the sea!" he cried, and if the cook had not opened his arms to catch him, he would have fallen to the deck.

The cook was a Frenchman and very probably a Gascon, as his name was François Tapage. He spoke English like a Yankee.

"Come, get up," said he, addressing the negro with a vigorous kick.

"Master Tapage!" cried the poor devil, throwing despairing glances toward the propellers.

"Well, Frycollin."

"Does this thing ever break?"

"No; but the time will come."

"Why? How?"

"Because, as they say in my country, '*tout lasse, tout passe, tout casse.*'"

"But the sea is below us."

"So much the better for us in case we fall."

Frycollin wriggled into the cabin and fell flat on the floor, his face down.

During the day the air-ship traveled at only a moderate rate of speed, and kept an average height of about one hundred and ten feet above the surface of the sea below it.

Uncle Prudent and his companion had withdrawn to their cabin and did not meet Robur, who was promenading the deck, sometimes alone, sometimes with George Kerns. Only about one half of the propellers were working, and sufficed to support the machine in the lower strata of the atmosphere.

On the surface of the sea below them the sentinel sighted a number of whales, of that white-bellied species that attain a length of seventy to seventy-five feet. This species of whale is the most redoubtable cetacean of northern seas, and are of such power and strength that even professional whalers often hesitate to molest them. There is no danger, however, in harpooning them from a height of over a hundred feet, and the crew of the "Albatross" were making preparations for the sport. The massacre was cruel and useless; but Robur wished by conquering one of the monster cetaceans, to show to the two members of the Weldon Club another exhibition of the powers of the "Albatross."

At the cry of "There she blows!" Uncle Prudent and Phil Evans came out of their cabin, thinking that there might possibly be some whaler in sight, and resolved, in that case, to throw themselves into the sea and take their chances of being rescued.

The crew of the "Albatross" were already ranged along the deck.

"All ready?" asked Foreman Kerns.

"All ready," replied Robur.

In the turrets, the engineer and his two assistants were at their posts ready to execute the maneuver at signs from Robur.

The "Albatross" was lowered to a height of fifty feet above the sea.

Several jets of water soon announced the presence of whales coming to the surface to breathe. George Kerns and one of the crew had stationed themselves in the bow. Kerns was armed with a huge gun, throwing a javelin bomb.

Robur had mounted on the quarter deck at the bow of the machine, and directed the movements by signals, his right hand for the engineer and his left for the steersman. He was thus master of the air-ship in all directions, horizontal and vertical, and it obeyed his commands with won-

derful precision and incredible rapidity. One might have called it an organized being of which Robur was the soul.

"There she blows!" shouted George Kerns, as the back of a whale appeared at some distance in front of the "Albatross."

George Kerns brought his gun to his shoulder and fired, and the projectile, carrying a long cord, struck the body of the whale. The bomb, filled with fulminating material, exploded and threw out a two-pronged harpoon, which buried itself in the flesh of the cetacean.

"Attention!" cried Kerns. Uncle Prudent and Phil Evans were, in spite of themselves, becoming interested in the spectacle. The wounded whale struck the water with his tail with such force that the spray was scattered over the passengers of the "Albatross," and then plunged into the depths of the ocean. The line attached to the harpoon flew out with such speed that it was necessary to keep a constant stream of water pouring on it to prevent combustion. The whale returned to the surface and started toward the north, drawing the "Albatross" with it.

George Kerns stood at the bow, hatchet in hand, ready to cut the line should a new plunge of the whale prove dangerous.

For half an hour and over a distance of six miles the "Albatross" was thus towed, but the strength of the cetacean was evidently failing.

Then, at a sign from Robur, the engineer reversed the screws, and the machine commenced to exert its power against the whale, which was little by little drawn closer to the "Albatross," and in a few minutes was struggling in

the water twenty-five feet below the air-ship. The powerful tail was still thrashing the water and producing large
whirlpools around it.

Suddenly the whale gave a frantic leap, and plunged
below with such rapidity that George Kerns had not time
to cut the line. In an instant the air-ship was dragged to
the surface of the ocean, into the whirlpool formed by the
disappearance of the cetacean, and the water poured over
the ramparts on the deck.

Fortunately, with a blow of the hatchet, George Kerns
severed the cord, and the "Albatross," freed from its burden, raised up to its former height.

Throughout the dangerous situation Robur had maintained his customary calmness, and had maneuvered the
machine with extraordinary coolness.

Some minutes after the whale returned to the surface—
this time dead, and its aerial destroyer resumed its flight to
the west.

At six o'clock, the morning of the 17th of June, the
profile of a country outlined itself in the horizon. It was
the peninsula of Alaska and the Aleutians; and they were
passed during the day and following night. Behring Sea
was quickly crossed, and the course of the "Albatross"
appeared to head toward China and Japan, and the morning of the 19th the "Albatross" reached the Strait of La
Perouse, separating Japan from the Saghalien Islands.

A thick fog closed around the air-ship, drenching with
vapor everything on board. At the height at which it was
running there was no danger of collision with mountains
or other obstructions, and the fog did not, therefore,

hamper the movements of the "Albatross," but the moisture of the atmosphere was disagreeable. The action of the suspensive screws was increased, and the "Albatross," rising some hundred feet, cleared the fog and pursued its flight in clear air.

As the "Albatross" rose, the hopes of Uncle Prudent and Phil Evans fell, as they had calculated that on reaching Japan the air-ship would lower its flight and present an opportunity for escape.

A few minutes later, as Robur was passing by them, he stopped for an instant and said:

"Gentlemen, allow me to point out to you another advantage possessed by an air-ship over a sailing vessel or a steamship. In the midst of such a fog as we have just conquered a ship would have been almost helpless, and would have crept slowly along in constant danger of a collision. You have just seen the method by which the 'Albatross' defies the thickest fog, and I think you will admit that the plan is an admirable one," and Robur calmly continued his promenade without awaiting their reply.

"Uncle Prudent," said Phil Evans, "it seems that this astonishing 'Albatross' fears nothing."

"We shall see," responded the president of the Weldon Club. The fog lasted during three days, hiding from view the country beneath the passengers, but on the 22d the mist cleared away, and they saw below an immense city of palaces, villas, gardens and parks.

Robur recognized the city without seeing it, by the barking of myriads of dogs, the cries of birds of prey, and above all by the sickening odor of decaying bodies.

The two colleagues were leaning over the rail, endeavoring to discover the name of the city, when Robur addressed them:

"Gentlemen, I see no reason why I should hide from you the fact that at this moment you are over the city of Yeddo, the capital of Japan."

Although this was precisely what they were trying to find out, Uncle Prudent replied: "We see no reason to conceal from you the fact that to the best of our knowledge we have made no inquiry of you concerning the name of this place."

"I imparted the information gratuitously," answered Robur, "and to it will add that in a short time you will also see Pekin!"

Nothing could be more amiable.

During the night indications of a rapidly approaching typhoon arose, sudden falling of the barometer, disappearance of vapor, large clouds massing themselves in the depths of the copper-colored heavens; in the opposite horizon long dashes of carmine were vividly traced on a slate-colored background; the sea was calm and still, but in the rays of the setting sun the water threw back a somber scarlet color.

Very fortunately the typhoon turned to the south; and the two members of the Weldon Club escaped witnessing a combat with the only element capable of coping with the "Albatross." In an hour the Corean Strait was freed and while the typhoon was beating against the south-eastern shores of China the "Albatross" balanced itself over the Yellow Sea. During the 22d and 23d of June, the

Gulf of Petcheli rolled beneath the air-ship, the 24th it crossed the valley of Pei-Ho and at last hovered above the capital of the Celestial Empire.

From their position on the deck the two colleagues were able to obtain a distinct view of the immense city, of the wall dividing it into two parts, the twelve suburban towns surrounding it, the large streets radiating from the center, the temples with their green and yellow roofs bathed in the light of the morning sun, the parks surrounding the houses of the mandarins, the pagodas, imperial gardens, artificial lakes, and in the center of the city the imperial palace, a fantastical wealth of wonderful architecture.

At this moment the air surrounding the " Albatross " was filled with a singular harmony. It sounded like a concert of æolian harps.

The air was filled with kites formed of party-colored paper and light strips of bamboo cut into different lengths. The wind rushing between these strips produced a mournful melody which ranged throughout an entire octave and formed a melancholy harmony.

Robur desiring a closer hearing of the aerial orchestra, the " Albatross " slowly descended toward the earth.

The approach produced an extraordinary effect on the excited populace below.

Deafening blows of tam-tams and other formidable instruments of the Chinese orchestra, firing of pistols, cannon and bombs, all intended to frighten off the air-ship. If the Chinese astronomers recognized the machine as the mysterious apparition which a month previous had occasioned so much controversy, the other Celestials, from the

humblest water-carrier to the many-buttoned mandarin,
took it for a hideous monster usurping the sky of Buddha.
The cords attached to the kites were cut or quickly drawn
in and some of them fell rapidly to the earth, while others
fluttered down like wounded birds chanting their death-
songs.

A powerful blast from George Kerns's trumpet sounded
over the city and smothered the last notes of the aerial
concert, but did not interrupt the terrestrial fusillade.

A bomb burst about twenty feet from the machine,
and the "Albatross" ascended higher into the inaccessible
zones of the sky. During the succeeding three days no opportunity to escape presented itself to the two prisoners.
The course of the air-ship laid directly to the south-west,
and pointed toward Hindoostan. Twelve hours after leaving Pekin Uncle Prudent and Phil Evans caught a glimpse
of the great wall at the extremity of Chen-Si. Then,
avoiding the Loung Mountains, they passed over the Valley of the Whang-Ho, and crossed the boundary line between the Chinese Empire and Thibet.

Thibet—with its high plateaus devoid of vegetation,
here and there snowy peaks, parched ravines, glacier-fed
torrents, shallow ponds over glittering salt beds, and lakes
hid in the depths of immense forests. The barometer indicated a height of twelve thousand feet above the sea,
and although it was the warmest season of the year in that
country, the thermometer fell below zero, and the two colleagues found their cabin more comfortable than the deck.

The 27th of June, Uncle Prudent and Phil Evans saw,
cutting the horizon before them, an enormous barrier

which was crowned with some high peaks covered with snow. They braced themselves against the turret at the bow to resist the air, as the "Albatross" was flying against the wind, and attentively scrutinized the colossal mass which seemed to block the path of the air-ship.

"Undoubtedly the Himalayas," said Phil Evans, "and it is probable that Robur will turn their base without trying to cross into India."

"So much the worse," replied Uncle Prudent. "Once in India, our chances for escape would be better."

"Unless he turns the chain on the east into Burmah, or on the west into Nepaul. Unless he adopts either of these courses he can not reach India."

"Indeed?" said a voice behind them.

The next day, the 28th of June, the "Albatross" found itself over the province of Zang. On the other side of the Himalayas was India.

The two colleagues came from their cabin and found the crew at their posts, Robur standing at the bow, and George Kerns with his hand on the steering apparatus, carefully executing the maneuvers of the machine, as it rose swiftly higher and higher into the heavens. The falling barometer indicated a height of 24,500 feet. Suddenly the suspensive screws were stopped, and the "Albatross" descended in an oblique direction, and Robur left his post at the bow and advanced toward his guests.

"Gentlemen, India."

CHAPTER X.

IN WHICH WILL BE SEEN HOW AND WHY FRYCOLLIN WAS TAKEN IN TOW.

ROBUR did not intend to continue his flight over the marvelous country of Hindoostan. His sole desire in clearing the Himalayas was to show the powers of his machine, and to convince those who did not wish to be convinced. Uncle Prudent and Phil Evans did not allow the admiration they must have felt to appear, as all their thoughts were directed toward escaping. They did not even admire the superb spectacle offered to their view as the "Albatross" followed the picturesque borders of the Punjaub.

The morning of the 29th of June they reached the incomparable valley of Cashmere, and a few hours after crossed the town of Srinagar, better known under the name of Cashmere. The "Albatross" stopped over the lake, and descending to within thirty yards above the water, remained stationary. Then, by means of a rubber tube, George Kerns replenished the supply of water, which, during the long flight, was nearly exhausted. During the operation Uncle Prudent and Phil Evans were interested spectators. The same thought had flashed through their brains. They were but a few yards above the surface of the lake. They were both good swimmers. A plunge would set them free, and once in the water, how could Robur recapture them? The propellers beneath the "Albatross" would be useless, as they would be submerged.

In an instant all the chances *pro* and *con* presented themselves to their minds, and in an instant they had weighed them. A quick leap and they were on the handrail; another leap and several hands grasped them and pulled them back to the deck.

They had been watched and their attempt at escape foiled. Robur had stood calmly by during their maneuver and contented himself by saying:

"Gentlemen, when guests have had the pleasure of voyaging on the 'Albatross' in company with Robur the Conqueror, they do not leave him so abruptly. Their departure is attended with more ceremony."

Phil Evans dragged away his colleague, who was about to commit some act of violence, and they entered their cabin dejectedly.

The "Albatross" resumed its course to the west, and during the day cleared the country of Cabulistan and reached the frontiers of Herat.

In the country over which they were now speeding there appeared to be large gatherings of men, convoys, artillery, and, in a word, everything constituting the *personnel* and material of an army on the march. They could also hear at times the booming of cannons and the cracking of musketry. But the inventor did not mingle with the affairs of others, except where it was a question of honor or humanity.

If Herat, as has been said, is the key to Central Asia, it mattered little to him whether the key was in a British or a Muscovite pocket. The daring spirit that claimed the air for its unique domain troubled not itself with terrestrial affairs. The country began to disappear under a storm that was frequently produced in these regions, and the "Albatross" was forced to ascend higher into the air. The Persian frontier faded from view, and early on the morning of July 2d the high peak of Damavend, with Teheran at its base, was sighted.

The "Albatross" passed over the city about ten o'clock in the morning, and a rapid view of the shah's palace and its magnificent gardens was obtained. The course of the "Albatross" was changed to the north, and some hours after found itself over a little city on the banks of a stretch of water that extended north and south as far as the eye could see. The city was the port of Ashourada, the furthest station south belonging to Russia.

The water was the Caspian Sea.

During the morning George Kerns had been chatting with the cook, François Tapage, and in reply to a question had remarked: "Yes, we shall stop over the Caspian Sea about forty-eight hours."

"Good," replied the cook. "We shall have an opportunity to fish."

This conversation was overheard by Phil Evans, who, without their knowledge, had been standing behind them and who would probably have gained further information had not Frycollin broken in with his customary morning litany of fright. Finding that nothing further was to be learned Phil Evans hurried to Uncle Prudent's cabin and acquainted him with George Kerns's words.

"Phil Evans," said Uncle Prudent, "we should no

longer deceive ourselves as to the intentions of this wretch."

"No," replied Phil Evans. "He will set us at liberty when it suits him—if he ever does."

"Consequently our own efforts must set us free from this 'Albatross.' "

"Which we must admit is a famous machine."

"Possibly so," returned Uncle Prudent, "but it is the machine of a scoundrel, who holds us here against all right, and therefore this machine constitutes for us and others a permanent danger. If we can end by destroying it—"

"Let us commence by saving ourselves," responded Phil Evans. "We shall see to the other afterward."

"So be it," replied Uncle Prudent, "and now let us profit by the present occasion. After leaving the Caspian the 'Albatross' will probably head over Europe, possibly to the north over Russia or to the west over Austria. If we can escape then, our safety is assured. We must get everything ready for the hour."

"But how can we reach the ground?" demanded Phil Evans.

"Listen to me. There are times during the night when the ' Albatross' flies at a few hundred feet above the earth. There are several ropes on board of that length, and with a little courage we might slide down."

"Yes," responded Phil Evans, "it may be done, and for my part I do not hesitate to attempt it."

"Nor I," said Uncle Prudent. "I have noticed that

4

during the night no one is on watch except the steersman
at the stern.   Now, if one of these ropes is concealed in
the bow during the day it would not be impossible to un-
coil it at night, unseen and unheard.''

"Nothing easier," said Phil Evans.   "I see with pleasure, Uncle Prudent, that you are calm, and that is a strong
point in our favor.   But here we are, over the Caspian
Sea, and a number of vessels in sight.   The 'Albatross'
will descend to fish.   Shall we profit by the occasion to—''

"To be seized again as we were just a short time ago.
They must undoubtedly be watching our movements even
now," responded Uncle Prudent.

"But that does not say that our movements are also followed during the night," said Phil Evans.

"During the night, then, we will carry out our plans
and finish with this 'Albatross' and its master.''

The two colleagues, Uncle Prudent in particular, were
growing desperate and ready to resort to any means to
secure their freedom.   A sense of their helplessness, the
ironical disdain with which Robur treated them, his brutal
manner of answering their questions, all tended to aggravate their situation, which day by day became more un-
bearable.

That very day a new scene occurred that led to a re-
grettable altercation between Robur and the two colleagues.
Frycollin, as usual, was the cause of the dispute.   Finding
himself over a vast sea, out of sight of land on all sides,
the poltroon had a fresh attack of fright.   Like the coward
that he was, he began to moan, protest, cry and to twist
his trembling body into a thousand shapes.   "I want to

get off—let me down," he cried. "I am not a bird; let me down; let me down."

It is unnecessary to say that Uncle Prudent made no efforts to calm him. On the contrary, he seemed to enjoy the scene, probably thinking that the yells and screams would annoy Robur. George Kerns and his companions were ready for their fishing operations, and to rid himself of Frycollin Robur ordered one of the crew to lock the nuisance up in his cabin. But the negro continued his clamor, kicking at the door and howling louder than ever.

"Attention," cried George Kerns, who had just harpooned a large fish, which looked like a young shark. It was a magnificent sturgeon, seven feet long, of the Russian species, the eyes of which, mixed with salt, vinegar, and white wine, are made into caviare. The balance of the crew turned their attention to drawing in the nets, and François Tapage's eyes sparkled as carp, salmon, and salt-water pike were poured on the deck in hundreds. An hour's work sufficed to fill the larder and the air-ship resumed its course to the north.

During the halt Frycollin had not ceased from yelling and thumping the door of the cabin in which he was confined, keeping up an unsupportable hubbub.

"Will that unhappy negro ever stop?" said Robur, finally, out of patience.

"It seems to me, sir, that he has a right to complain," said Phil Evans.

"Yes, and I also have the right to rid my ears of this nuisance," replied Robur.

"Captain Robur!" said Uncle Prudent, just appearing on deck.

"President of the Weldon Club!"

The two men advanced until but a few paces apart, and looked straight into each other's eyes.

For a minute Robur returned Uncle Prudent's gaze, then, shrugging his shoulders, he said:

"Bring a rope."

George Kerns comprehended, and Frycollin was dragged from the cabin. His cries of terror were redoubled as the foreman and one of his comrades seized him and bound him in a sort of basket, to which they firmly tied the end of a rope. It was one of the same ropes that Uncle Prudent hoped to make use of. The negro was afraid he was about to be hanged, whereas he was only to be suspended. The cable was let out to a distance of one hundred feet, and Frycollin found himself balanced in space. He could cry at will now. But fright had paralyzed his larynx and he was dumb. Uncle Prudent and Phil Evans attempted to oppose the proceedings, but they were repulsed.

"It is infamous, it is cowardly," cried Uncle Prudent, white with rage.

"That is a matter of opinion," retorted Robur.

"It is an abuse of power against which I protest."

"Protest."

"And for which I shall be revenged."

"As you please."

"Both on you and yours."

The crew of the "Albatross" had approached, awaiting a sign from their master, but Robur motioned them back.

"Yes, on you and yours," repeated Uncle Prudent, his colleague vainly endeavoring to quiet him.

"I am at your service," answered Robur.

"You shall be forced to regret your cowardice and rascality."

"Enough!" said Robur, in a menacing tone. "There are more ropes on board, and the method which has quieted the valet may also teach a lesson to the master."

Uncle Prudent was almost suffocating with anger, and raved like a frantic man. Fearing the consequences, Phil Evans carried him bodily into the cabin and held him there until he cooled off.

In the meantime the weather during the past hour had undergone considerable modification, and a storm was brewing. The atmosphere was charged with electricity to such a degree that at half past two Robur witnessed a phenomenon that he had never observed before. In the north, from which direction the storm was coming, luminous scrolls of vapor were rising, caused by the passing of the electric current through the different strata of clouds. The reflection of these electric clouds ran along the surface of the sea in myriads of lights, which grew brighter as the heavens darkened. And Frycollin? Well, Frycollin was still in tow—and tow is the correct word, for the speed of the air-ship was throwing the rope into a pronounced angle, and Frycollin and his basket were some yards in the rear.

His fright may be judged, when the lightning commenced to furrow through the space around him, while the thunder claps pealed in the depths of the heavens.

The "Albatross" was running at its usual height, about

three thousand feet, when a deafening clap of thunder
rolled immediately around them. The squall broke suddenly, and in a few seconds the clouds of fire had closed
around the "Albatross."

Phil Evans started to intercede in behalf of Frycollin
and to beg that he might be drawn on board. But Robur
had anticipated the request and the rope was already being
hauled in, when all at once there was an inexplicable
slackening in the rotation of the suspensory screws. Robur
leaped to the central turret.

"Put on more speed," he cried to the engineer; "we
must rise out of the storm at once."

"Impossible, captain."

"Why?"

"The current has broken."

The Albatross was sinking slowly. As often happens
with the current of telegraphic lines during storms, the
supply of electricity was decreasing in the accumulators of
the air-ship. In telegraph matters this means only a delay
in transmitting dispatches; here, in this case, it was a
frightful danger, which meant that the air-ship would be
cast helpless into the sea.

"Down, down," cried Robur, "and out of this electric
zone. Come, my men, keep cool."

Robur mounted on his quarter-deck and the crew stood
at their posts, ready to execute the orders of their master.
The "Albatross," although it had dropped some hundred
yards, was still buried in the electric cloud, with the lightning
playing around it, like a piece of fire-works. The danger
of their situation was increasing. The suspensive screws

were working slower and slower, and what was then an easy descent threatened to change to a rapid fall. In less than a minute they would reach the surface of the sea, and, once submerged, no power could draw them from the abyss.

Suddenly they cleared the fiery mass and the electric cloud floated above them. The Albatross was but sixty feet above the crest of the waves, and in two or three seconds they would be drowned like rats in a cage.

But Robur had embraced the few seconds which presented themselves, and leaping to the central turret seized the lever and shot out the full power of the current of the batteries, no longer neutralized by the electric tension of the atmosphere. In an instant the propellers regained their normal speed, stopped the fall, and the "Albatross" glided away, leaving the storm behind it.

It is useless to say that Frycollin had taken a forced bath. When he was drawn on board he held as much water as a sponge. The next morning, July 4, the "Albatross" had cleared the Caspian Sea.

CHAPTER XI.

UNCLE PRUDENT OPENS A LINE OF COMMUNICATION WITH THE EARTH.

IF ever Uncle Prudent and Phil Evans had almost abandoned the idea of flight it was during the succeeding fifty hours. Robur knew now that they had determined to escape, and took extra precautions to prevent them. Any attempt on their part now would have been suicide. When one leaps from an express shooting along at a rate of sixty miles an hour he risks his life, but when the speed is almost one hundred and twenty miles an hour it is certain death.

For some time the wind had been coming from the northeast and the course of the " Albatross " laid to the west, going with the wind. But as the wind calmed it became difficult for the passengers to stand on deck, and their respiration was interrupted by the rapidity of their flight against the air. At one time they were compelled to brace themselves against their cabin to escape being thrown to the deck. The steersman, looking through the windows of their cage, perceived their predicament, and the " Albatross " was slowed up sufficiently to permit the two colleagues to regain their cabin.

The last city that had been passed was Astrakhan, situated at the northern extremity of the Caspian Sea. The Star of the Desert, as some Russian poet has called it, has fallen from the first to the fifth or sixth magnitude. The two colleagues, in their rapid flight, had caught a glimpse of the town beneath, with its old battlement-crowned walls, the antique towers in the center of the city, and its five-domed cathedral, a mass of ancient architecture.

It was ten o'clock in the morning, July 4, when the air-ship pointed to the north-west, following the lines of the Volga River.

The Ural steppes stretched out on either side of the river. At last in the evening the air-ship flew over Moscow without stopping to salute the flag over the Kremlin. In ten hours the "Albatross" had crossed the one thousand two hundred miles between Astrakhan and the old capital of all the Russias.

From Moscow to St. Petersburg the line by railroad is not more than seven hundred and twenty miles, about an easy six or seven hours' trip for the air-ship, and the "Albatross" reached the Neva and St. Petersburg at two in the morning, and during the next ten hours had crossed the Gulf of Finland, the Baltic Sea, Sweden and Norway. Finally, when over the famous Rjukanfos falls in Norway, the course of the "Albatross" was suddenly changed to the south.

During this long and wonderful flight, Frycollin remained quietly in his cabin, sleeping as best he could, except at meal times, which he attended with his customary promptitude. François Tapage visited him at intervals and appeared to thoroughly enjoy the negro's fright.

"Well, my boy," asked he, during one of his visits, "how is it you do not cry now? It is a pity you are not in the basket now, as at the rate we are now going there is an excellent draught of air for your rheumatism."

"This bird is going to pieces, and we are lost," groaned Frycollin.

"Perhaps it is, my brave Fry, but we are going so fast that we can not fall."

"Do you think so?"

"On the word of a Gascon."

In truth the "Albatross" was then flying with such rapidity that the action of the suspensory screws was almost un-

necessary. The air-ship was shooting through the air like a
Congreve rocket.

"And will this thing last for a long time?" asked Frycollin.

"Well, not very; only for a life-time."

The valet recommenced his lamentations.

"Take care, Fry; remember the basket," said the cook,
and Frycollin, trembling like a leaf, crammed a napkin into
his mouth and was quiet.

In the meantime Uncle Prudent and Phil Evans, who
were not the men to waste valuable time in useless recriminations, were discussing their situation. It was now evident to them that escape was difficult, not to say impossible. At the same time, if they were unable to themselves
set foot again on the terrestrial globe, was it not possible
to acquaint the inhabitants with the events that had transpired since their disappearance, the manner in which they
had been captured and held as prisoners on the "Albatross," and in this way excite their friends to some action
that might free them from Robur's clutches?

How could they correspond with the earth below?
Would it suffice to imitate the method used by shipwrecked
sailors, who write their names and whereabouts on a slip of
paper, inclose it in a bottle and throw it in the sea? But
here in this case the sea was the air. Unless the bottle
struck some person below, the chances were that it would
not be found. And in case the bottle did strike some one
below, the chances are that it would fracture his skull, and
render the two colleagues open to a charge of manslaugh-
ter. But the two members of the Weldon Club were des-

perate, and nothing else on board offering itself as suitable for their purpose they had decided to use a bottle, when Uncle Prudent suggested another plan. Uncle Prudent, as we know, was a snuff-taker, and as a matter of course owned a snuff-box, which was now empty. The snuff-box was made of aluminium and stronger than a bottle. Once thrown out of the "Albatross." it might be discovered by some honest citizen, who would carry it to the bureau of police, where they would take charge of the document which made known the situation of the two victims of Robur the Conqueror.

The work was soon performed. The note was short, but told all, and, giving the address of the Weldon Club, requested that the document should be forwarded to that institution.

Then Uncle Prudent inclosed the note and wrapped the snuff-box up in thick bands of linen, to break the force of the fall on the earth. There was nothing further but to await a favorable opportunity to cast the box over the side unobserved. In reality this was the most difficult part of the operation, as ever since their attempt to escape they were closely watched. Besides, they had to take precautions against throwing the box into any sea or lake.

The "Albatross," after leaving Norway, had headed toward the south, following the line of longitude which forms the meridian of Paris, and crossing over the North Sea, not without astounding and terrifying those on board the thousands of vessels plying between England, Holland, France and Belgium. No use of sending down their message now, and the two colleagues were obliged to wait for a more

favorable moment. However, an excellent occasion was
soon presented.

At ten o'clock that evening the "Albatross" reached the
shores of France. The night was very dark. For an instant they could see the light-house of Gris-Nez on one side
of the Calais strait mingling its electric rays with the Dovel
light, which towered on the other side, and the "Albatross"
crossed the coast into the French territory, maintaining a
height of three thousand feet. The speed had not been
moderated. The air-ship darted like an arrow over the
cities, towns and villages, so numerous in the rich provinces
of Northern France. The meridian of Paris was closely
followed, the course lay in a straight line, and shortly after
midnight the "Albatross" flew over the "City of Light,"
which merits its name even at the hour when its inhabitants are or, rather, ought to be in bed. By some strange
fantasy Robur was prompted to make a halt over the
French capital, and the "Albatross" descended to within
a few hundred feet of the city. Robur and the crew left
their cabins to breathe the fresh, soft air that was blowing
across the deck, and Uncle Prudent and his companion,
recognizing the admirable opportunity to accomplish their
design, also appeared on deck. They endeavored to isolate
themselves from the crew, as it was necessary that their
actions should escape observation.

The "Albatross," like a gigantic beetle, slowly crossed the
great city, following the boulevards brilliantly illuminated
by Edison lights. They could hear the sound of carriage
wheels rumbling over the streets and the puffing of the
trains on the tracks coming into Paris from all sides.

Then the air-ship passed from the steeples of the Trocadero
to the metal tower of the Champ du Mars, whose enormous
reflectors bathed the capital in a flood of electric light.

This aerial promenade, or nocturnal stroll, lasted for
about an hour. Robur resolved to give the astronomers of
Paris a sight of a meteor which they had not predicted.
The air-ship's electric lights were started into activity.
Two streams of dazzling light played on the squares, gardens, palaces and the sixty thousand houses of the city, and
great waves of light swept from one horizon to the other.

The "Albatross" was seen, not only seen, but heard as
well, for a triumphant blast from George Kerns's trumpet
sounded over the astonished city. At this moment Uncle
Prudent, leaning over the side, opened his hand and let the
snuff-box fall.

In a few minutes the "Albatross" ascended rapidly.

Then into the heights of the Parisian heavens rose an
immense hurrah from the already large crowd assembled
on the boulevards—a hurrah of stupefaction addressed to
the fantastic meteor mounting the sky above them. Suddenly tho lights of the air-ship were extinguished, and surrounded by darkness and silence, the "Albatross" took up
its route to the south.

By four o'clock France had been crossed obliquely, and
in order not to lose time by crossing the Alps or Pyrenees,
the "Albatross" rounded the Cape Antibes, over the surface
of Provence. At nine o'clock the Italians gathered at St.
Peter's were astounded at the sight of the huge bird flying
over the "Eternal City." Two hours after, over the Bay
of Naples, it balanced itself for an instant among the

fuliginous clouds of Vesuvius, and at one o'clock, after cutting the Mediterranean Sea, it was detected by the inhabitants of Tunis.   After America, Asia; after Asia, Europe.   During the past twenty-three days the "Albatross" had flown over eighteen thousand miles.   And now it was starting into the explored and unexplored regions of Africa.

*   *   *   *   *   *   *

It may prove interesting to know what became of the famous snuff-box after its fall.

The box fell into the Rue de Rivoli, in front of No. 210, at a time when the street was deserted.   The next morning it was found by an honest street sweeper, who carried it in all haste to the prefect of police.   The prefect, with the natural timidity of his calling, took it for an infernal machine, but finally mustered up courage to unroll the bandage and open the box.   A document was found inclosed, which to their surprise read as follows:

"Uncle Prudent and Phil Evans, president and secretary of the Weldon Club, of Philadelphia, are imprisoned in the air-ship "Albatross," commanded by the inventor, Robur.

"Communicate this to our friends and acquaintances.
                                                "U. P. and P. E."

The nature of the phenomenon was at last explained to the inhabitants of the two worlds, and calm restored to the scientists and astronomers of the observatories scattered over the surface of the terrestrial globe.

CHAPTER XII.

UNCLE PRUDENT DESIRES TO FIGHT A DUEL.

AT this stage of the "Albatross's" voyage of circum-navigation, it is permissible to put the following questions:

Who is this Robur, whose name is all that we know concerning him? Has all his life been passed in the air? Has he not a retreat in some inaccessible place in which, if his machine does not need repose, it can at least revictual? It would be surprising if this was not the case, as even eagles have eyries.

Most important of all, what was his intentions toward his prisoners? Was he determined to hold them in his power, condemned to perpetual airation? Or, after carrying them over Africa, South America, Australasia, the Indian, Atlantic, and Pacific oceans, would he set them free, saying, "Now, gentlemen, I trust you will admit the claims of the ' heavier than air.' "

To these questions it is still impossible to reply. It is the secret of the future, and will perhaps one day be solved. As regards his nest, Robur was not seeking it, at all events, in the northern frontiers of Africa. He satisfied himself with passing the remainder of the day over Tunis, flying or hovering at will over the surrounding country. Shortly afterward he started for the interior, threading the valley of the Medjerda, following the cours' of its yellow waters over thickets of cactus and roses.

During the night the "Albatross" balanced over the
frontiers of Kroumire, and there was not a Kroumir who
that night did not fall with his face to the ground and in-
voke Allah's protection against the gigantic eagle. The
flight over Algeria lasted throughout the next day, and the
course of the "Albatross" was changed to the southeast.
The following morning the steersman from his cage saw
the morning star twinkling over the sands of the Sahara.

Approaching the desert the "Albatross" regained the
higher zones of the air to escape the blinding sheets of
sand that the blast of the simoom was throwing up like the
spray of the ocean. Then followed the desolate plateaus
of Chebka, stretching out in black lava-strewn plains to
the fresh and green valley of Ain-Massin.

Before night some hundred miles had dropped in their
rear. If the "Albatross" had desired to make a halt it
would have landed now in the oasis of Ouargla, which, almost hidden beneath a forest of palm-trees, stretched beneath them. They could plainly see the town, the old
palace of the Sultan, the brick houses tinged with a cop-
pery red under the rays of the declining sun, and the
artesian wells bored in the valley, where the air-ship might
replenish its liquid supply. But, thanks to the extraordinary speed of the "Albatross," the water-tanks, which were
filled at the Valley of Cashmere were still amply supplied.

Had the "Albatross" been seen by the Arab, Mozabite
and negro inhabitants of the oasis of Ouargla? It must
have been, for it was saluted by a number of musket
shots, the balls refalling to the earth before reaching the
"Albatross."

Then night came on, that silent night in the desert whose secrets have been so poetically revealed to us by Felicien David.

During the following hours the air-ship turned to the southwest, crossing the route to El Golea, discovered in 1859 by the intrepid Frenchman, Duveyrier. The darkness was profound. Nothing could be seen of the Trans-Saharian Railway then in course of construction, a long band of iron reaching from Algiers to Timbuctoo, through Laghouat, Gardaia, and finally reaching the Gulf of Guinea. Crossing the Tropic of Cancer the " Albatross " entered the equatorial regions.

At 600 miles from the northern frontiers of the Sahara it cleared the route where Major Laing found his death in 1846, and cut across the caravan road running from Maroc to Soudan. A single incident occurred during the morning. A cloud of locusts darkened the air and fell on deck in great quantities, threatening to swamp the air-ship.

George Kerns and his men were kept busy clearing the deck, and in some time had rid the platform of the winged nuisances, excepting a few hundred, which were saved by François Tapage. And he prepared them in so savory a manner that Frycollin stopped trembling long enough to ejaculate:

" These shrimps are good. "

They were now at the northern boundary of the immense kingdom of Soudan and 110 miles from the oasis of Ouargla. At two o'clock in the afternoon they could see a city in the distance, situated at the bend of a large river.

The river was the Niger. The city was Timbuctoo.

If, until then, that African Mecca had only been visited by the travelers of the Old World, Imbert, Adams, Laing, Caille, Barth, and Lenz, that day by the chance of their singular adventure, two Philadelphians, if ever they returned to their beloved city, would be able to speak of it from three standpoints, visual, auditory and olfactory.

Visual, because they could see the triangular city stretching beneath them; auditory, because it was a great rête day and they were making a great ado with their celebrations; olfactory, because their olfactory nerves were very disagreeably reminded that the "Albatross" was then over the square of Youbou-Kamo, where the king's dining-hall was situated.

The inventor did not intend that the president and secretary of the Weldon Club should remain in ignorance of the fact that they were contemplating the Queen of the Soudan, now in the power of the Touarey nation.

"Timbuctoo, gentlemen," said he in the same tone in which he twelve days previous had said, "India, gentlemen."

Then he continued:

"Timbuctoo, latitude 18 degrees north, longitude 5 degrees 56 minutes west of the meridian of Paris, 745 feet above the level of the sea. Important city of from twelve to thirteen thousand inhabitants, a city celebrated in ancient times for progress in science and art. Perhaps you would like to stop over for a few days?"

Robur was evidently in a humorous mood. He went on:

"But that would be dangerous for strangers to attempt in that mass of negroes, Berbers and Arabs, more particularly as they would probably be displeased at our arrival on air-ship."

"Sir," replied Phil Evans, in the same tone, "to have the pleasure of leaving you we would willingly accept our chances of being badly received by these natives. Prison for prison, and better Timbuctoo than the 'Albatross.'"

"That is only a matter of taste," replied the inventor. "But at all events I shall not try it, as I hold myself responsible for the safety of the guests who do me the honor of traveling with me."

"So, Captain Robur," said Uncle Prudent, going off at half-cock, as usual, "you are not content with being our jailer. To this wrong you must also add insult."

"You mistake my intention."

"Are there any weapons on board?"

"Yes, a complete arsenal."

"Two revolvers will suffice, if I hold one, sir, and you the other."

"A duel!" cried Robur; "a duel which would result in the death of one of us."

"Which must end in that manner."

"No, Mr. President, no. I prefer to hold you alive."

"Perhaps you are more desirous of your own safety. That is wise."

"Wise or not, it suits me best. You are free to think as you please and to act in whatever manner you can."

"We have already acted."

"Indeed."

"Was it so difficult while crossing the inhabited portions of Europe, to let fall a document—"

"You did that?" asked Robur, stirred by an irresistible impulse of rage. "If you did, you have merited—"

"What?"

"To follow your document over the rail."

"Throw us over, then," cried Uncle Prudent, "for we have thrown over the paper."

Robur advanced toward the two colleagues. At a gesture from their captain, George Kerns and some his comrades drew around the colleagues. The inventor was seriously tempted to put his threat into execution, and, afraid to trust himself, he precipitated himself into his cabin.

"Good!" said Phil Evans.

"And what he does not dare to do I will do myself," shouted Uncle Prudent. "Yes, I will do it myself."

At this time the population of Timbuctoo were massing themselves in the squares and filling the streets with excited crowds, while the priests from the minarets of their temples launched the most violent maledictions against the aerial monster. Had the "Albatross" descended to the earth it would have been torn to pieces. For some miles the "Albatross" was escorted by shrieking ibis and storks who flew by the side of the air-ship, but were soon distanced.

Through the night the air was filled with the trumpeting of elephants and the roars of the lions prowling through the surrounding country. The morning of the 11th passed the mountains separating the Soudan from the Gulf of Guinea, and the profile of the Kong Mountains, situate in the kingdom of Dahomey, appeared in the horizon. Since leaving Timbuctoo, Uncle Prudent and Phil Evans noticed that their course had laid directly south, and they concluded that if the course was not altered the air-ship would soon reach the equinoctial line. Would the "Albatross" then abandon the continent and launch itself not over a Behring Sea, a Caspian Sea, or a Mediterranean Sea, but over the great Atlantic Ocean?

The prospect did not please the two colleagues, whose chances for escape would be considerably diminished. The "Albatross" made a slight turn in its course, as if it hesitated to leave the African country. Was the inventor thinking of retracing his flight? No. But his attention was specially drawn to the country over which he was passing. We know, and he also knew it, that the kingdom of Dahomey is one of the most powerful countries on the Western coast of Africa.

Although strong enough to successfully combat with its neighbor, the Ashantee nation, the limits of the country are nevertheless restricted, only counting 120 leagues from the north to the south, and 60 leagues from east to west, but its population comprises 800,000 souls, taking in the territories of Ardrah and Wydah. If the kingdom of Dahomey is not large, it is, however, notorious. It is noted for the frightful cruelties which mark its annual fêtes, by the sacrifice of human lives to the terrible hecatombs, perpetrated in honor of a dying king and his successor. When the King of Dahomey receives a visit from a foreign embassador, it is considered a high mark of courtesy to present the stranger with a few dozen heads struck off in his honor—struck off by the Minister of State, the "Minghan," who also executes the duties of the headsman creditably

At the time the "Albatross" crossed the frontier of
Dahomey, the King Bahodon had just died and the entire
population were preparing to assist in the celebration attending the inauguration of his successor. There was
from this fact a great excitement through the country, an
excitement that had escaped Robur's observation. In fact,
long columns of natives could be seen traveling from the
country toward Abomey, the capital of the kingdom.
Well-beaten roads crossing vast plains covered with giant
plants, immense fields of manioc, magnificent forests of
palm-trees, cocoanut-trees, mimosas, orange-trees, and
mangoes; such was the country whose perfume was wafted
up to the "Albatross" and through which parrots and
cardinal birds were flying by thousands.

The inventor was stationed at the bow, leaning over the
rail absorbed in his reflections, and at intervals exchanging
a few words with George Kerns. The "Albatross" did
not appear to be noticed by the moving masses below,
often hidden under the impenetrable tops of the trees. At
11 o'clock in the morning the "Albatross" hung directly
over the city, and the passengers could see the wall circling
the town, the deep trenches extending around it, large
trees regularly laid out on the level soil, and the large
square surrounding the king's palace. The houses of the
city are overlooked by a large terrace, situated a short distance from the place of sacrifice. During the fête days it
is from this terrace that the prisoners inclosed in wicker
baskets are thrown to the people, who furiously tear the
unfortunates to pieces.

In a section of the court surrounding the king's palace,

4,000 warriors are quartered, one of the contingents of the royal army and the most courageous one. If the presence of Amazons in the regions of the river of that name is doubted, it can not be denied that they exist in Dahomey.

Some of them are clothed in white tunics, blue or red scarfs, white trousers striped with blue, and white caps, and armed with guns and knives; others, the elephant hunters, are armed with heavy carbines and short-bladed swords, this class being clad in tunics of blue and red, and caps of white; and the battalion of young girls in blue tunics and white caps, are true vestals, pure as Diana, and like their goddess armed with bows and arrows. When one sees in addition to the Amazons, 5,000 or 6,000 male soldiers arrayed in white trousers, blue caps, and with parti-colored scarfs knotted at their shoulders, he can form an idea of the appearance of the army of Dahomey.

Abomey was that day entirely deserted. The king and his suite, the masculine and feminine army, and the entire population had left the capital and were assembled without the city on a vast plain surrounded by magnificent woods. There on that plain the celebrations in honor of the new king were to take place. It was there that thousands of prisoners were to be immolated before night. It was about two o'clock when the " Albatross " arrived over the plain and commenced to descend, surrounded by a few clouds which still hid it from the eyes of the natives.

At least sixty thousand people were gathered below on the plain, attracted from all parts of the kingdom, Widah, Kerapay, Ardrah, Tombony, and the more distant villages.

The new king—a vigorous fellow named Bou-Nadi—about twenty-five years old, occupied a little hillock well shaded by the branching trees.

Around him pressed his new court, his male army, his amazons, and all his people. Immediately around the hillock fifty or sixty musicians were squatted, making the air hideous with their barbarous instruments, tambours of asses' skin, guitars, gourds, pounding brass bells with iron hammers, and flutes of bamboo shrilly sounding over the *ensemble*. Then, at intervals, discharging of fire-arms, firing of cannons and bombs; in short, such an uproar that a clap of thunder would scarcely have been heard through the deafening clamor.

In a corner of the plain, guarded by the soldiers, were the mass of captives who were elected to accompany the defunct king into the other world, one of the privileges of royalty, and to the obsequies of Ghozo, father of Dahadou, his son had contributed 3,000 companions. During an hour there were speeches, harangues, palavers, together with dances, executed not only by the alluring bayaderes, but by the Amazons as well, who deported themselves with a war-like grace.

But the hour for the hecatomb approached. Robur, who was acquainted with the bloody customs of the country had not lost sight of the prisoners—men, women and children—who were to be devoted to the slaughter. The Minghan held himself ready at the foot of the hillock, where the king was seated, brandishing over his head a short-bladed sword of ponderous weight. This time he was not alone. Around him were grouped a hundred headsmen, who, through long practice, could decapitate a body at a single blow.

In the meantime the "Albatross" was slowly approaching, coming down obliquely and moderating the action of its screws. It soon emerged from the clouds which had hidden it until within 300 feet from the earth, and for the first time it was seen.

The ferocious natives who ordinarily would have been terrified at the apparition, now flushed with their excitement, took the air-ship for a celestial being descending to do homage to King Bahadou.

There arose an indescribable enthusiasm, interminable appeals, noisy supplications, general prayers, all addressed to the supernatural hippogriff who, they thought, was coming to transport the body of the defunct king into the highest realms of the Dahomian heavens. The first head rolled from under the saber of the Minghan, and the prisoners began to fall by hundreds under the weapons of his bloody assistants.

Suddenly a rifle cracked on the deck of the "Albatross."

The Minister of Justice fell, his face to the ground.

"Well aimed, George," said Robur.

"Bah! He is only the first of a thousand who will follow," replied the foreman.

His comrades, armed with rifles, were ready to fire at a signal from Robur.

A sudden change operated in the crowd below. They were beginning to comprehend the true state of affairs.

This winged monster was not a friendly spirit, it was a spirit hostile to the good people of Dahomey.

At the fall of the Minghan cries of vengeance arose from the plain, and a general fusillade was directed toward the air-ship.

These menaces, however, did not prevent the "Albatross" from descending to within 150 feet from the soil.

Uncle Prudent and Phil Evans, notwithstanding their strained relations with Robur, felt bound to co-operate with him in the work of humanity he was about to perform.

"Let us deliver the prisoners," they cried.

"That is what I propose to do," responded Robur.

The repeating rifles in the hands of the two colleagues and the crew of the air-ship began a steady fire, not a ball being wasted in the midst of the human mass below. The cannon on the deck was pointed toward the crowd and cut long furrows at every shot. Very soon the prisoners, without recognizing the quarter from which aid was coming, began to break their bonds, while the soldiers were returning the "Albatross's" fire. The interior propeller was penetrated by a ball and several other projectiles buried themselves in the turrets.

"Ah, they must have it, then," cried George Kerns. and, hurrying to the ammunition stores, he returned with a dozen dynamite cartridges, and distributed them among the crew. At a sign from Robur the cartridges were thrown into the crowd, and, striking the earth, exploded like shells.

The army and populace, at this fresh form of attack, were

seized with panic, and broke for cover, the prisoners scattering to all quarters without any one pursuing them.

Such is the manner in which the fêtes in honor of the new King of Dahomey were disturbed, and Uncle Prudent and Phil Evans were shown a new phase of the powers of the air-ship and of the service it might render to humanity.

The "Albatross" tranquilly ascended higher into the air and pursued its course, leaving Wydah far behind, and in a few hours the waves of another ocean rolled beneath it.

The Atlantic Ocean.

CHAPTER XIII.

UNCLE PRUDENT AND PHIL EVANS CROSS AN OCEAN WITHOUT BEING SEASICK.

YES, the Atlantic.

The fears of the two colleagues were realized.

Robur did not seem to exhibit the slightest concern at crossing the vast stretch of water, and since the night of the 14th of July, the "Albatross" had been speeding above the Atlantic Ocean. The next morning when day broke the sun rose in that circular line where the sky and water met. No land in sight within the vast field of vision.

Africa had disappeared in the northern horizon.

When Frycollin ventured from his cabin, when he saw the sea below him, his old-time terror again seized him. *Below* is not exactly the proper word, *around* him would better describe it, for, to one elevated to such a height, the abyss appears to literally surround him at every point, and the circular horizon is constantly receding.

Frycollin possibly could not have explained this sensation physically, but he felt it morally. It sufficed to produce in him that "fear of the depths" which attacks men otherwise brave.

However, the negro spent no time in analyzing his sensations. With his eyes tightly closed he groped his way into his cabin with the intention of remaining there for a long time. The most recent work of meteorologists, based on considerable observation, has established the fact that in the intertropical regions the trade winds meet, sometimes near the Sahara and sometimes near the Gulf of Mexico.

The equinoctial line had been crossed the 13th of July, and Uncle Prudent and Phil Evans learned that they had passed from the northern to the southern hemisphere. The crossing of the line was not attended with the celebration and ceremony which accompany the operation on the men-of-war and merchantmen sailing the waters below.

François Tapage alone contented himself with pouring a quart of ice-water down Frycollin's back, but as the baptism was followed by several glasses of gin the negro declared himself ready to cross the line as many times as they wished him to, provided it was not on the back of a mechanical bird.

The morning of the 15th the "Albatross" flew between the Ascension Island and Saint Helena, the mountains of the latter having appeared in the horizon a few hours previous. It is certain that had there existed such a machine as Robur's during the period when Napoleon was in the power of the English, Hudson Lowe, in spite of his insulting precautions, would have experienced the chagrin of seeing his illustrious prisoner escape, *via* the air line. During the evenings of the 16th and 17th a curious phenomenon was produced at sunset. At a higher latitude it would have been mistaken for the aurora borealis. The setting sun projected long, many-colored rays, tinging the air around with a vivid green. Some few scientists have attempted to explain the phenomenon by attributing it to the reflection of the sun on particles of dust floating in the air, but had they been on the air-ship these savants would have admitted their error.

Close examination proved that the air held in suspension numerous crystals of pyrites, vitreous globules and minute particles of iron, all analogous with the matter thrown out by volcanoes. There was no doubt but that the crystaline particles had been thrown out by a volcanic eruption, and were held in suspension over the Atlantic by the aerial currents.

The 18th of July another phenomenon manifested itself, which would have terrified the captain of a sailing vessel.

A rapid succession of luminous waves swept over the surface of the ocean at a speed estimated by Phil Evans of nearly sixty miles an hour. These waves tore along about eighty feet apart, tracing long furrows of light.

As night came on the reflection glared up to the "Albatross," and the sea below looked like a mass of fire, fire without heat.

The phosphorescent light was produced by the presence in the water of myriads of animalculæ emitting the strange and brilliant light which lit up the waters for miles around.

The 47th southern parallel was now passed, and the days which were now only seven or eight hours long, were decreasing in length as the air-ship approached the Antarctic regions. At about two o'clock in the afternoon the "Albatross" was lowered to reach a more favorable current of air, and flew along about one hundred feet above the sea.

The weather was calm. In the sky above the "Albatross" a large cloud was forming, the center bulging out in the direction of the ocean. The water, under some mysterious influence, seemed to be attracted upward toward the cloud. Suddenly the water leaped up, taking the shape of an enormous bladder. In an instant the "Albatross" was enveloped in the whirl of a gigantic waterspout. Happily, the gyratory motion of the waterspout was opposed to that of the suspensive screws, otherwise, the air-ship would have been drawn into the sea; and even as it was the machine was already revolving with incredible rapidity.

The danger of their position was incalculable, since Robur was powerless to disengage his machine from the suction of the water-spout, which retained its hold in spite of the propellers. The crew, thrown across the deck from side to side, were endeavoring to grasp the supports to prevent themselves going over the side.

"Keep cool!" shouted Robur. They were obliged to keep their patience also.

Uncle Prudent and Phil Evans, who were just leaving

their cabin when the air-ship was struck, were thrown to the stern and almost went over the side.

"Load the cannon!" cried Robur.

The order was addressed to George Kerns, who was hanging to the little piece of artillery mounted in the center of the deck, where the centrifugal force was least felt. The foreman understood Robur's design. Instantly he seized a cartridge from the caisson, threw open the breech of the cannon, and slipped in the cartridge.

The report sounded above the roar of the whirlpool, and the water-spout broke.

The concussion of the air had sufficed to break the mass of water, and the enormous cloud above, resolving itself into rain, streaked the horizon with immense liquid threads uniting the sea and sky. The "Albatross," freed at last, quickly ascended higher into the air.

"Anything broken on board?" asked Robur.

"No," replied George Kerns; "but I think the turning put a few extra twists into Frycollin's wool."

For fifteen minutes the "Albatross" had been imperiled and owed its safety to its extraordinary strength, without which it would have been destroyed. During their passage across the Atlantic the hours seemed very long unless the monotony was relieved by some exciting incident like that which had just occurred. Nevertheless, the days were steadily decreasing in length, while the cold was increasing.

Uncle Prudent and Phil Evans saw but little now of Robur. Closed in his cabin, the inventor was engaged the larger portion of the time in laying out the route, marking on his charts the direction to be followed, taking observations of his position, noting the indications of the barometers and thermometers, and entering on his log-book the incidents of the voyage. The two colleagues, well muffled and hooded, kept a constant watch at the bow, waiting for the sight of some land in the South. By the express command of Uncle Prudent, Frycollin was endeavoring to obtain from the cook some clew to Robur's identity.

François Tapage proved worthy of the Gascon blood flowing through his veins. Robur was formerly the Minister of State of the Argentine Republic, a lord of the British Admiralty, a President of the United States living in retirement, an exiled Spanish general, a viceroy of the Indias, who, seeking a more exalted position, found it in the air. Once upon a time he was worth millions, but he started a newspaper. He was then compelled to make public ascensions to regain his fortunes. As to whether his captain was ever going to settle down on the earth, the cook felt obliged to answer that he was not.

But then it was his intention to visit the moon, and if he found the surroundings to his liking he was going to locate there.

"Ah, Fry, my comrade, how pleased you will be when you wake up some fine morning, and find yourself in the moon."

"I will not go—I refuse," answered the imbecile, taking it all seriously.

"And why not, Fry—why not? We will marry you to some young and beautiful Lunarian, and you will be the founder of a race of negroes."

And when Frycollin reported this conversation to his

master, Uncle Prudent saw that it was impossible to obtain any information relating to Robur; and he now directed his efforts toward vengeance.

"Phil," said he one day to his colleague, "it is very clear now that escape is impossible."

"You are right."

"So be it; but a man is always his own property, and if by sacrificing his life he can also—"

"If the sacrifice is to be made let it be made quickly," replied Phil Evans, whose temper, cool as it was, was being sorely tried. "This thing must and shall end—where is the 'Albatross' going now? Here it is crossing the Atlantic Ocean obliquely, and if it maintain its course, will strike the coast of Patagonia, and then Terra del Fuego, and after this? Will he head his course over the Pacific Ocean, or toward the continent around the South Pole? Everything is possible to this Robur. At all events, we are lost. It is a case of legitimate defense, and if we must perish—"

"We shall not do so before we are avenged, without having destroyed this machine and all on board."

The two colleagues had worked themselves up to the highest pitch of fury. Since it was necessary, they were resolved to sacrifice themselves to destroy the inventor and his works. In a short time there would be no one left alive to tell the story of the wonderful air-ship, the king of aerial locomotion. Notwithstanding the fact that the idea had buried itself deeply into their minds they had not yet thought of the means to execute their design.

How were they to do it? By secreting an explosive

5

engine under the deck and blowing the air-ship up? In
that case it would be necessary to gain access to the ammunition room.   Fortunately, Frycollin knew nothing of
these projects.   At the thought of the "Albatross" ex-
ploding in the air he would have denounced his master.
July 23d land was sighted in the south-west, close to Cape
Virgins, at the entrance to Magellan Strait.   At that time
of the year, at the 54th parallel, night lasted almost eighteen hours, and the temperature frequently fell to six or
seven degrees below zero.   The "Albatross," instead of
turning off to the south, followed the windings of the
strait as if wishing to reach the Pacific.

After passing over Lomas Bay, leaving Mount Gregory
on the north and the Brecknock Mountains on the west, it
reached Punta Arena, a little Chilian town, and some
hours later sighted the old station of Port Famine.   If the
Patagonians, whose fires could here and there be seen,
were, as is reported, above the ordinary stature, the passengers on the air-ship could not appreciate the fact, as
the people below seemed to them like dwarfs.

During the few short hours of the southern day a magnificent spectacle was afforded them.   Abrupt chains of
mountains, peaks tipped with eternal snow, thick forests
growing on the mountain-sides, interior seas, bays formed
between peninsulas, and the archipelago comprising Clar-
ence, Dawson and Desolation Islands, channels and passes,
all forming a confusing medley which the ice was already
uniting into one solid mass, from Cape Forward, the ter-
minus of the American continent, to Cape Horn, the ter-
minus of the New World.

In the meantime, after reaching Port Famine, the "Albatross" changed its course to the south. Passing between Mount Tarn, on the Brunswick peninsula, and Mount Graves, it headed toward Mount Sarmiento, an enormous peak, hooded with ice, towering over Magellan Strait, six thousand feet above the level of the sea. It was the country of the Fuegans, the natives who inhabit the "land of fires." Six months previous, the height of summer (January in Philadelphia), the days fifteen or sixteen hours long, the country would have appeared beautiful and fertile. They could see even now valleys and pastures extensive enough to nourish millions of animals, old forests, gigantic trees, birch, ash, beech, cypress and arborescent ferns; also vast armies of penguins, gulls and myriads of other species of birds.

At night when the electric lights of the "Albatross" were suspended, gulls, ducks, geese, and other sea-birds cast themselves by thousands on the deck.

As the sun went down, about three o'clock in the afternoon, they could see a vast lake circled by a superb forest. The lake was frozen over, and the natives on snow-shoes were gliding over the surface. At the sight of the air-ship the Fuegans were fleeing in all directions, and where they could not flee they burrowed into the ground like animals.

The "Albatross" maintained its southerly course, passing Beagle Channel, then Navarian Island, whose Greek name contrasts strangely with the ruder names of these far-off lands; then Wollaston Island, washed by the last waters of the Pacific. At last, after having cleared since leaving the coast of Dahomey over 4200 miles, the "Al-

batross" darted over the most southern extremity of the
new world. Below, battered by an eternal surf, lay the
terrible Cape Horn.

CHAPTER XIV.

IN WHICH THE "ALBATROSS" DOES THAT WHICH PERHAPS NEVER HAS BEEN DONE BEFORE.

THE next day was the 24th of July. The 24th of July
in the southern hemisphere is the 24th of January in the
northern. Further, the 56° of latitude had just been
passed, and this degree corresponds to the parallel which
in the north of Europe crosses Scotland at Edinburgh.
The thermometer held itself constantly below zero, the
artificial means were necessary to heat the interior of the
cabins and turrets on the air-ship.

The length of the days was still diminishing as the "Albatross" drew nearer to the Polar regions. The air-ship
flew over that portion of the Pacific Ocean confined within
the Antarctic Circle. The cold was growing more and
more intense, and it was necessary to dress after the fashion of Esquimaux or Fuegans. The two colleagues, well
muffled, were constantly on deck, always dreaming of their
scheme and watching their opportunity to execute it.
Now and then they met Robur, but since the threats exchanged between them at Timbuctoo not a word had
passed between them.

As to Frycollin, he did not venture out of the kitchen,
where François Tapage accorded him generous hospitality

—provided Frycollin performed the duties of assistant cook. To what point was the "Albatross" heading? Did Robur dare to venture in the depth of winter over the southern seas washing the pole? Would the chemical agents of his batteries prove strong enough to resist congelation? That Robur would attempt to clear the pole during the warm season the two colleagues well knew, but to do so, surrounded by the continual night of the Antarctic winter, was the act of a fool.

Thus reasoned the president and secretary of the Weldon Club, of Philadelphia, who were now but a few miles below America, but, to their sorrow, many thousand miles from their beloved Walnut Street.

The 24th of July the captain held frequent consultations with his foreman. At times he and George Kerns consulted the barometer, not only to gain an idea of their height, but to notice the approaching state of the weather.

Something of importance was transpiring.

Uncle Prudent also noticed that Robur took an inventory of the provision stores on board and of the supplies for the engines of the propulsive and suspensive machines. This seemed to him an indication of an early return.

"A return?" said Phil Evans. "What for?"

"To the place where Robur revictuals his air-ship," replied Uncle Prudent.

"That ought to be some lonely island in the Pacific, peopled by scoundrels worthy of their chief."

"Exactly so, Phil. I believe that now he will bear off

to the west and, putting on all speed, reach his destination
as soon as possible."

"But we can not carry out our plan if he reaches it."

"He shall not reach it, Phil."

The two colleagues had partly divined the inventor's
plans, for during the day the "Albatross" took a retrograde course, and, after advancing some sixty miles fur
ther south, suddenly turned to the west.

The liquid plain stretched out below them, from America to Asia, took on a singular aspect. Under the feeble
rays of the winter sun which struggled through the semi-
night surrounding the air-ship the surface of the Pacific
Ocean was of a milky white. The waters looked like a
vast field of snow, and had the entire surface of the sea
been frozen over the sight would not have been different.

We know that the phenomenon is produced by the presence of luminous particles and phosphorescent animal-
cules, but it is surprising to meet with the opalescent mass
in any water but the Indian Ocean.

Suddenly the barometer, which for several days had
been steadily rising, fell rapidly, symptoms which might
have troubled a sailing vessel, but which the air-ship did
not deign to notice. Evidently some great storm had
swept over the Pacific and gave signs of bursting anew.
Shortly after noon George Kerns approached the captain
and said: "Captain Robur, can you see that black speck
in the horizon? There—directly north from us. Is it a
rock?"

"No, George, there is no land in that direction."

"Then it is a ship, or perhaps a boat."

Uncle Prudent and Phil Evans, who were standing in the bow, looked toward the direction indicated by George Kerns.

Robur called for his marine glass, and after carefully scrutinizing the object, said:

" It is a boat, and there are men on board. "

" Shipwrecked sailors?" cried Kerns.

" Yes, castaways, forced to abandon their sinking vessel; unfortunates who have lost their reckoning and may be dying of hunger and thirst. Well, it must not be said that the ' Albatross ' refused to save them."

Robur gave an order to the engineer, and the air-ship commenced to slowly descend.

When within three hundred feet of the water it stopped, the propellers were started, and the " Albatross " shot rapidly to the north, and soon reached the boat. No air was stirring, and the improvised sail hung limp on the mast, the crew evidently too weak to use the oars.

In the bottom of the boat five men were stretched out asleep, or overcome with fatigue.

The " Albatross " slowly lowered over the sleeping crew.

At the bow of the boat was the name of the abandoned ship—the " Jeannette," from Nantes.

" Halloo!" shouted George Kerns, at the top of his voice.

As the air-ship was about seventy feet above, his cry should have been heard.

No response.

" Fire a musket," said Robur.

The order was executed, and the report rolled over the waters.

One of the castaways raised himself painfully, his eyes haggard and bloodshot, his face and figure emaciated as a skeleton.

Seeing the fantastic shape of the air-ship above, he fell back with a gesture of terror.

"Fear nothing," cried Robur, in French. "We are here to save you. Who are you?"

"Sailors of the 'Jeannette,' a three-masted bark, of which I was mate. Our vessel sprung a leak and was sinking when we left it, fifteen days ago. For the last four days we have been out of water and provisions."

The other sailors were, one by one, reviving. Haggard, exhausted and wasted to shadows, they stretched out their arms to the "Albatross."

"Attention!" cried Robur. A cord was thrown over the side, and a bucket of fresh water lowered to the boat. The unfortunates threw themselves on the bucket and drank with feverish haste.

"Bread, bread!" they cried.

Then a basket containing food, conserves, a flask of brandy and several pints of coffee, was lowered to the sailors.

It was seized and rapidly emptied by the famished men. Then:

"Where are we?"

"Fifty miles from the coast of Chili and the Chonos Archipelago," answered Robur.

'But there is no wind, and—"

"We will tow you."

"Who are you?"

"Men who are happy to have aided you," replied Robur, simply.

The sailor recognized and respected an incognito. The boat, attached to the air-ship by a long rope, was drawn toward the east, and at ten o'clock that evening land was sighted, or rather the fires which denoted the presence of land.

The castaways of the "Jeannette" could attribute their safety to a miracle. After conducting the boat to the entrance of the Chonos Islands, Robur cried to them to throw off the rope, which they did with cries of gratitude for their benefactor, and the "Albatross" started for the open sea.

During the next day the air-ship maintained its rapid flight, and the following morning crossed the limits of the Polar Sea, having cleared since leaving Cape Horn over thirteen hundred miles.

There, during the month of July, the nights were twenty hours long, and the sun only appeared in the horizon to, in a short time, disappear again. At the Pole the night is prolonged to seventy-nine or eighty days.

If observations could have been taken that day they would have shown that the air-ship was only fourteen hundred miles from the Antarctic Polo.

Uncle Prudent and Phil Evans did not for an instant quit the deck, where they were now able to remain undisturbed by the resistance of the air, which in the polar regions was still and quiet. The domain around the Southern Pole comprises four million five hundred thousand square meters. Is it a continent, an archipelago or a frozen sea? That question is, as yet, unanswered.

But it is well known that the Southern Pole is consider

ably colder than the Northern, owing to the position of the earth in its orbit during the Antarctic winter. The "Albatross" had entered the polar regions at the sixty-fifth meridian; by what meridian would it go out? As it kept up its southern course the days grew shorter, and in a short time it plunged into that perpetual night only lit by the light of the moon or by the pale rays of the southern aurora borealis. But the moon was new, and Robur's companions were unable to view the region whose secrets still escapes human curiosity.

The "Albatross" very probably passed some points already discovered. Graham's Land, found in 1832 by Biscoe, and Louis Philippe Land, discovered in 1838 by Dumont d'Urville. The temperature was yet very low, but not cold enough to occasion suffering, as there seemed to be a current of air which, like an aerial gulf stream, carried with it a certain amount of heat. It is to be regretted that the region was plunged into profound darkness. Even had the rays from the moon been more powerful partial observations might have been afforded the passengers. Besides, at that period of the year, an immense sheet of snow, a frozen mantle, covered the surface of the country, obliterating the outlines.

Under these conditions how could they distinguish the form of the country, the stretch of the seas, disposition of the islands, or the hydrographical tracings of the region. It was equally impossible to gain any knowledge of the orographical configuration, as mountains and hills were confused with icebergs and glaciers. Shortly before midnight an aurora borealis lit up the shadows.

With its silvery fringing rays darting across space, it took the form of an immense fan opened in the heavens. Its longest rays seemed to reach the Southern Cross and lose themselves in the light of the four stars glittering in the zenith.

It goes without saying that during the flight to the South Pole the compass needle had been curiously affected, and gave no precise indication of the direction followed by the air-ship. Nevertheless Robur, aided by his more delicate instruments, was able to relatively fix his location.

Shortly after midnight he appeared on deck and, glancing at the compass, which now ceased to fluctuate, and comparing it with the memoranda of calculations formed from the other instruments, he remarked to George Kerns: "The South Pole is beneath our feet."

This was the fact scientifically, but nothing could be seen through the darkness, and it was left to their imaginations to believe the fact that they were then above the spot where all the meridians of the globe meet and cross. A strong current of wind had risen and was blowing with startling force. Had the "Albatross" encountered a mountain now the machine would have been crushed like an egg-shell.

The magnetism of the pole rendered the electric machinery useless. The summit of a broken chain of mountains suddenly raised some distance off. The dangerous position of the air-ship was heightened by the fact that the wind was to the east, and a collision with the mountains was imminent. Two luminous points showed themselves in front of the "Albatross," about thirty miles off.

They were two volcanoes, parts of the vast systems of Mounts Ross, Erebus and Terror.

Would the " Albatross, like a gigantic butterfly, fall a victim to the flames which were darting up before it?

It was an hour of fear and suspense. One of the volcanoes—Erebus—already seemed to loom up before the air-ship, which the current of air was bearing swiftly on. Sheets of flame leaped up from the crater, and a curtain of fire barred their way. The deck of the air-ship was brightly illuminated with the vivid glare, and the forms of the crew looked like demons, standing like statues, without a cry, without a gesture, waiting for the terrible moment when they would be enveloped in the fiery furnace.

But the storm that carried the " Albatross " along also saved them from that frightful catastrophe. The flames of Erebus were beaten down by the tempest, and the " Albatross " passed over a shower of lava which was fortunately repulsed by the centrifugal force of the suspensive screens which after leaving the Pole began to work. An hour after, two colossal torches in the horizon behind the air-ship lit up the long polar night. At two o'clock in the morning, Ballery Isle was passed, and then the " Albatross " passed out of the Antarctic circle, cutting the one hundred and sixty-fifth meridian.

The storm was still carrying the air-ship along, threatening a hundred times to dash it to pieces against the numerous icebergs floating on the ocean. The " Albatross " was no longer in the hands of the steersman, but in the hands of God—and God is a good pilot.

At last crossing the sixtieth parallel, the storm gave signs of abating, and as it decreased in violence the "Albatross" commenced to become master of itself. Then, as it regained the higher altitudes of the earth, day began to appear at the civilized hour of eight o'clock in the morning. Robur and his machine, after narrowly escaping a cyclone while rounding Cape Horn, were at last freed from the storm.

They had darted through the Pacific Ocean from a point near Cape Horn to the South Pole, clearing the distance of twenty-one hundred miles in nineteen hours. Robur was now ignorant of his whereabouts, as the compass was still charged with the magnetism which had affected it at the South Pole. It became necessary to rely on observations of the sun, but during the entire day the skies were darkened with huge clouds and the sun did not appear.

This was a disappointment which was increased by the fact that the two propelling screws had been damaged during the storm.

The speed of the air-ship was necessarily diminished, and it was moving slowly, about eighteen or twenty miles an hour. It was necessary to guard against further damage, for if the two propellers were to become entirely disabled, the air-ship above the vast Pacific would be placed in a most dangerous situation. Robur resolved to descend in some secluded spot and repair the damage.

The next morning, July 27th, at seven o'clock, land was sighted in the north. They could see that the land was an island, but which of the thousand isles that dot the Pacific it was they could not tell. Nevertheless, Robur decided to stop there; one day would suffice to repair the damage, and they could depart the next.

The wind had calmed and was favorable for the operation of descending over the island. If there had been a strong gale blowing, the "Albatross" might have wasted a week in seeking to alight. A rope five hundred feet long attached to an anchor was dropped over the side. When the air-ship reached the side of the island the anchor trailed through the breakers and finally fixed itself firmly between two rocks. The cable stretched taut for an instant under the strain of the suspensive screws, and the "Albatross" floated in the air like a ship at anchor. It was the first time it had been connected with the earth since its departure from Philadelphia.

CHAPTER XV.

A FEW THINGS TRANSPIRE HARDLY WORTH THE TROUBLE OF TELLING.

EVEN when the "Albatross" was yet high in the air the passengers could see that the island was but of mediocre size. But what parallel cut it; on what meridian was it situated? Was it an island of the Pacific, Australasian or Indian Ocean? Although the compass was not to be depended on, yet the general observations indicated that it was the Pacific. As soon as the sun appeared from behind the clouds the matter would be definitely settled. From their height, five hundred feet, the island, measuring about fifteen miles in circumference, was of triangular shape.

At the south-eastern extremity there was situated close to the shore a small isle, evidently the continuation of a chain of rocks which extended to the water's edge of the larger island.

At the north-west a conical mountain raised itself to a height estimated by the passengers at fourteen hundred feet. There were no signs of any inhabitants on the island, and if the place was inhabited the natives had probably taken flight at the approach of the air-ship. The anchor of the "Albatross" had caught in the rocks of the south-eastern end of the island, not far from where a stream emptied into the little bay.

While waiting to take his observations the inventor was preparing everything for the day's work. The suspensive screws were found to be in perfect condition, having worked admirably during the storm. But the two propellers had been damaged more seriously than Robur had imagined. It was necessary to unscrew the branches and repair the machinery which imparted the rotary motion.

The anterior propeller was now being repaired by the crew under the direction of Robur and George Kerns. This particular propeller was started upon first, for in case the "Albatross" should be obliged to leave before work was finished, they could dispense with that one easier than the other.

Uncle Prudent and Phil Evans, who had been promenading the deck, talking in an under-tone, were now seated at the stern. Frycollin was considerably reassured at finding himself only five hundred feet from the earth, and seemed in excellent spirits.

The work was only suspended for an instant to take the sun, which now shone clear and bright.

The result of the observation, made with the utmost exactitude, was:

Longitude: 176 degrees 17 minutes, west.

Latitude: 43 degrees 37 minutes, south.

Reference to the chart gave this position to Chatham Island and the Viff Islet, which form the group known as the Broughton Islands. The group is fifteen degrees east of Tawai-Pomanow, the meridional island of New Zealand, situated in the southern part of the Pacific Ocean.

"We are nearer than I supposed," said Robur to George Kerns.

"We are then—"

"Forty-six degrees, or twenty-eight hundred miles south of Island X."

"The more reason that we should repair our propellers," returned the former. "We have met with many contrary winds during our trip, and as our stock of provisions is running low it is necessary that we reach Island X as soon as possible."

"Yes, George, I hope to start during the night, using our single propeller and repairing the other on our way there."

"But these two gentlemen and their servant?" inquired George Kerns.

"They will be happy to become colonists of Island X," replied Robur. But where was this mysterious place?

An unknown island lying between the Equator and the Tropic of Cancer, an island which well merited the algebraic name which Robur had bestowed upon it. There Robur had founded his little colony; there the "Albatross" came to repose when fatigued with long flights; there it came to provision for long aerial voyages. On that Island X Robur, taking advantage of the natural resources, had established his work-yard and constructed his air-ship. He could here build and repair. His magazines held material, tools, supplies of every description, accumulated and operated by a few scores of inhabitants, the sole population of the island.

When Robur had doubled Cape Horn some days previous his intention was to reach the island by cutting obliquely across the Pacific, but the cyclone and storm had carried him into the polar regions. He had, however, only been carried a little way from his first course, and, had not the propellers broken, the delay would have been but trifling. But now to regain Island X. The distance was great, and they would probably have to fight contrary winds.

When night came on, the preparations would be completed and everything ready to cast off the anchor rope.

The crew, seeing that there was no time to lose, set rapidly to work to get the "Albatross" ready for the flight.

While the crew was working in the bow of the air-ship Phil Evans and Uncle Prudent were holding a conversation vital in its consequences.

"Phil Evans," said Uncle Prudent, "are you resolved, as I am, to sacrifice your life?"

"I am with you to the end."

"And for the last time, is it still evident to you that from this Robur we have nothing to expect?"

"Nothing."

"Then our course is clear. This night the "Albatross" leaves this island, and before this night is over we shall have accomplished our work. The wings of Robur's bird shall be broken. This night the air-ship will take a quicker leap through space."

"The time has come, and we will be avenged," replied Phil Evans.

It is clear that the two colleagues were in perfect accord in the matter which involved their own death, and which they viewed with indifference.

"Have we everything ready?" asked Phil Evans.

"Yes. Last night when Robur and the crew were fighting the storm, I slipped into the magazine-room and secured a dynamite cartridge."

"Let me have it. Quick!"

"No, no, you will ruin everything. Wait until to-night. When night comes we will enter our cabin where it is secreted, and we can then act without fear of surprise."

The two colleagues dined at six, after their habit. Two hours after they retired to their cabin, like men ready to pass the night in slumber.

Robur and his companions little suspected the danger that menaced the "Albatross."

In the conspirators' cabin Uncle Prudent was unfolding his story and plan.

As has been said, he had managed to gain entrance to the ammunition room, where he had obtained a quantity of powder and a cartridge, similar to those used by the inventor at the Dahomey massacre. Returning to his cabin, he had carefully secreted the cartridge with which he was resolved to blow up the "Albatross" while taking its flight through the air.

Phil Evans was examining the explosive engine obtained by his companion. It was a metallic bomb, containing over a pound of explosive mixture, sufficient to destroy the machinery and tear the air-ship apart. If the explosion did not destroy the "Albatross" at a single blow it would at least result in its fall. Nothing was easier than to place the cartridge in a corner of the cabin in such a manner that it would crash through the machinery and deck, vital parts of the air-ship. In order to explode the cartridge it was necessary to strike the fulminate cap with which it was furnished.

This was the most delicate part of the operation, as it was necessary to calculate precisely the minute for the explosion. Uncle Prudent had already provided for this, and formed his plans accordingly.

When the forward propeller was repaired the air-ship would take up its course to the north. This done, Robur and the crew would in all probability direct their attention toward repairing the posterior propeller. The presence of the crew around the cabin would necessarily hamper the movements of the plotters. That is why it was decided to employ a fuse to explode the cartridge at a given time.

Uncle Prudent unfolded his scheme to Phil Evans.

"At the same time that I secured the cartridge I also obtained a quantity of powder. With this powder I will make a fuse, regulating its length by the time it has to reach the fulminate cap. It is my intention to light it at midnight, and the explosion will follow between three and four in the morning."

"Well planned," replied Phil Evans.

The two colleagues were coolly arranging the details of a great catastrophe, in which they were to perish. They entertained such hate for Robur and his property that they did not hesitate to sacrifice their own lives to insure the destruction of the "Albatross" and all on board. The act was as you please—foolish or odious. Their five weeks of captivity had filled them with a rage that now reached its culminating point.

"And Frycollin," said Phil Evans, "have we the right to dispose of his life?"

"He must die with the others," responded Uncle Prudent.

Frycollin would doubtless have styled this reasoning defective.

Uncle Prudent immediately set to work, while Phil Evans kept close watch on deck. The crew were busy at the bow, and there was no fear of a surprise. Uncle Prudent reduced a small quantity of the powder to a fine state and inclosed it in a piece of linen, forming a fuse. He then lit a piece of the fuse, and assured himself that it would burn one and one half inches in ten minutes, of about a yard in three hours and a half.

The fuse was than attached to the cartridge, and at ten

o'clock in the evening the preparations had been completed without exciting the least suspicion.

Phil Evans rejoined his colleague in the cabin. During the day the work on the forward propeller had progressed rapidly, but required more time than was calculated. When night came on Robur and his crew stopped work and the propeller was not yet in position. After consulting with George Kerns, Robur had decided to give his crew a well-earned rest and to postpone the balance of the work until the morrow. Besides, it required daylight to properly adjust the delicate mechanism of the screw.

Uncle Prudent and Phil Evans were ignorant of this change. Relying on what they had heard from Robur they fancied that the work would be finished before night, and the "Albatross" would immediately take up its course to the north. They even now believed themselves freed from the island, whereas the machine was still held to the earth by the anchor-rope. This circumstance was soon to give an unthought of turn to affairs.

The night was dark, and the moon shining. Huge clouds rendered the obscurity more profound. A slight breeze was coming from the southwest, and the "Albatross" was swaying at the end of the cable connecting it with the island.

Uncle Prudent and his colleague were closed in their cabin, exchanging but few words and listening to the vibration of the suspensive screws, which surmounted all other sounds on board. They were waiting the time to act

A few minutes before midnight.

"It is time," said Uncle Prudent.

Under their couches there was a chest, where their clothing was kept. In this chest Uncle Prudent had placed the cartridge and fuse. There it could burn without betraying them by its odor and crackling. Uncle Prudent lit the end of the fuse. Then, pushing the chest under the couch:

"Now, to the stern, to wait for the end."

They reached the deck, and were surprised not to find the steersman at his habitual post.

Phil Evans leaned over the side and started back in amazement.

"The 'Albatross' has not moved," he said in a low voice. "The work was not finished."

Uncle Prudent made a gesture of disappointment.

"We must put out the fuse."

"No; we must save ourselves, responded Phil Evans.

"Save ourselves, how?"

"The anchor rope is here. A descent of five hundred feet is nothing."

"A trifle, Phil Evans, and we would be fools not to profit by the chance."

But they first returned to the cabin, securing everything they could carry that would be necessary during the prolonged sojourn on Chatham Island. Then they closed the door and noiselessly advanced toward the bow, intending to wake Frycollin and oblige him to follow them. The night was still dark, but the clouds were beginning to dissipate.

The air-ship was swaying the anchor rope, throwing it out of the perpendicular. The descent was difficult and dangerous, but what was that to men who a few hours age had not hesitated to throw their lives away. They glided softly over the deck, stopping now and then to listen carefully. Absolute silence reigned on board, save the whirr of the screws. It was not only silence, but deep slumber, into which the air-ship was plunged. Uncle Prudent and Phil Evans had almost reached Frycollin's cabin, when Phil Evans stopped short.

"The sentinel," said he.

A man was stretched out near the turret. If he was asleep, he was barely so. If he awoke, all escape was impossible.

Phil Evans cautiously crept back and returned with some ropes and a cloak.

The next instant the man was gagged, hooded and bound to one of the supports, unable to move or utter a cry.

The operation was performed with scarcely a sound. Uncle Prudent and Phil Evans listened; not a sound came from the interior of the cabins. All slept on board.

The two fugitives—they had now earned the name— reached the cabin occupied by Frycollin. François Tapage was giving vent to reassuring snores. Uncle Prudent reached out his hand to open the door. It was open. He stepped into the cabin. It was empty.

"There is no one here."

"No one there—where can he be?" murmured Phil Evans.

They turned to the bow, thinking that perhaps Frycollin was sleeping there in some corner. No Frycollin.

"Can the fool have divined our plan?" asked Uncle Prudent.

" Whether he has or not, we have done our duty, and can lose no more time. Let us be off. "

The two fugitives unhesitatingly grasped the rope between their hands, wrapped their`legs tightly around it, and, gliding down the cable, reached the ground, one after another, safe and sound.

They were filled with unspeakable pleasure at feeling beneath their feet the solid earth, and could have laid down and hugged the ground.

They were preparing to gain the interior of the island, and were about to cross the little stream, when a shadow rose before them.

It was Frycollin. Yes, the negro had watched his master's preparations for flight, and had the courage to precede him. Anything to reach the ground again.

But there was no time for recriminations, and Uncle Prudent was starting for the interior when Phil Evans stopped him:

" Uncle Prudent, listen to me. We are now here out of Robur's hands. In a short space of time he and his companions will meet with a horrible death, which they doubtless deserve. Be that as it may. But, if he will give us his word of honor not to seek to retake us—"

" The honor of a man like Robur is—" Uncle Prudent did not finish his sentence. Something was transpiring on the " Albatross. "

Evidently their flight had been discovered and the alarm given.

Some one was crying, " Help, help!"

The sentinel had freed himself from the gag. Hurried

steps sounded over the deck and the next moment the electric lights blazed down over the island.

"Quick! There they are," shouted George Kerns. The fugitives had been sighted.

Robur shouted out an order, and at the same time the suspensive screws slowed up, and the crew hauled in the cable, and the "Albatross" commenced to approach the earth.

At this moment Phil Evans' voice sounded clear above the confusion:

"Captain Robur, will you engage your word of honor to leave us at liberty on this island?"

"Never," cried Robur. And the reply was followed with a musket shot, the ball grazing Phil Evans' shoulder.

"Ah! the scoundrels!" cried Uncle Prudent, and, with knife in hand, he precipitated himself over the rocks to where the anchor was buried. The air-ship was but fifty feet above. The cable was instantly cut, and the wind, which had sensibly freshened, swept the "Albatross" into the north-east, compelling it to rise higher in the air.

————

CHAPTER XVI.

WHICH WILL LEAVE THE READER IN A REGRETABLE STATE OF INDECISION.

IT was twenty minutes past twelve. Five or six rifle shots had been sounded from the air-ship. Uncle Prudent and Frycollin, supporting Phil Evans, were sheltered behind the rocks. They were free, and for the time had nothing to fear.

The Albatross, when it was swept from Chatham Island, was carried to a height of nine hundred yards. It had been forced to ascend to keep from falling into the sea.

At the moment when the sentinel, freed from his gag, had uttered his first cry, Robur and George Kerns rushed from their cabins to his aid, and tore off the cloak which muffled him.

Then the foreman hastily ran to the cabin occupied by the two colleagues; it was empty.

François Tapage, for his part, had searched Frycollin's cabin; there was no one there.

Realizing that his prisoners had escaped, Robur was seized with a violent fit of rage. The escape of Uncle Prudent and Phil Evans was his secret, his personality, revealed to the world.

If the fact of their letting a document fall over Europe had not greatly disturbed him it was because that he believed it lost in the fall.

But now

Then calming himself:

"They have escaped; so be it. But they can not escape from Chatham Island, and in a few days, I will return—I will find them, and I will retake them. And then—"

The safety of the three fugitives was far from being assured. The "Albatross," once master of its movements, would make no delay in returning to Chatham Island. Before twelve hours the fugitives would again be in the power of the inventor. Before twelve hours! But before three hours had passed the "Albatross" would be destroyed.

The fuse was slowly and steadily nearing the dynamite

cartridge, and when it reached the end of its sputtering course the " Albatross " was doomed.

In the meantime the wind had quickened and the air-ship was carried to the north-east.

In order to return against the wind it was necessary that the forward propeller at least be completed.

" George," said the captain, " start on the electric lights."

" Yes, captain."

" And every man to work."

" It shall be done," replied the foreman.

No fatigue or postponing the work now. There was not a man in the crew but shared the anger of his chief, and was ready for any step to retake the fugitives.

As soon as the forward propeller was repaired they would return to Chatham Island and give chase to the prisoners. Then the rear propeller would be repaired and the air-ship could return in safety to Island X.

In the meantime it was important that the " Albatross " should not be carried too far to the north-east, and Robur experienced great difficulty in keeping the air-ship stationary.

Robur had not occupied his mind with the question as to whether the fugitives had been well received by the natives of the island, if there were any.

Whether these natives came to their assistance mattered little to him. With the means, offensive and defensive, at the disposal of the " Albatross," they would be promptly dispersed or annihilated. The capture of the prisoners was without question, and once retaken—

" They shall not escape from Island X," said Robur.

About an hour after midnight the forward propeller had been prepared. Nothing remained but to put it into place, which required another hour's work. This finished, the "Albatross" would return to the south-west.

But the fuse which was burning in the abandoned cabin; that fuse was more than a third consumed, and the spark was steadily nearing the cartridge. If the crew of the airship had not been otherwise occupied perhaps one of them would have heard the feeble crackling of the fuse. Perhaps he would have detected the odor of burning powder. It might have warned him, and he would have notified George Kerns or his captain. They would have instituted a search, and would have discovered the explosive engine. There was yet time enough to save the marvelous "Albatross" and those on board.

But the men were working at the bow of the air-ship, sixty feet from the abandoned cabin. Nothing called them to that part of the deck, nothing distracted them from the work which required all their attention. Robur was there also, working like the mechanic that he was. He hurried the work, without neglecting to see that all was performed with the greatest care. It was necessary to him, above all, that he should become again absolute master of his machine. If he did not retake the fugitives they would escape to their country. Investigations would be made, and Island X would not escape the search that would be made for it. That would be the end of the existence created by Robur for his crew.

At this moment George Kerns approached the inventor. It was quarter past one.

"Master Robur, I think the wind is abating and shifting a little to the west."

"What are the indications of the barometer?" asked Robur, after carefully observing the aspect of the sky.

"It is almost stationary, and the clouds are lowering about the 'Albatross,'" replied the foreman.

"Then we shall probably have rain. But no matter, that will not interfere with our work, as we will ascend above the clouds."

"If rain falls," replied George Kerns, "it will be but lightly—at least, I judge so from the appearance of the clouds—and it is probable that on clearing up the wind will calm."

"Undoubtedly, George, but I think it preferable not to descend yet. Let us finish repairing the damage, and we can then maneuver as best suits us."

A few minutes after two the first part of the work was completed. The forward propeller replaced, the batteries were started into activity. The movement of the air-ship accelerated and the "Albatross," headed to the south-west, returned with moderate speed in the direction of Chatham Island.

"George," said Robur, "we were drifted to the northeast during about two hours and a half. The direction of the wind has not changed, and in an hour at the most we will regain Chatham Island."

"I believe so, too," replied George Kerns, "for we are getting a good speed. Between three and four in the morning we will reach our point of departure."

"So much the better. We must reach there and even

land during the night and unobserved. The fugitives,
believing us far in the north, will not be on their guard.
We will endeavor to conceal ourselves under the higher
rocks of the island, and should we be compelled to remain
for some days—"

"We will remain," replied George Kerns, "and if we
have to fight against an army of natives—"

"We will fight them, George, we will fight for our
'Albatross.'" The inventor turned to the men, who were
waiting for new orders.

"My friends, it is not yet time for repose; we must
work till daylight."

They were ready now to commence operations on the
rear propeller, which had suffered the same damage from
the storm. To repair the propeller it was necessary to
stop the flight of the air-ship for a few minutes, and even
to assume a retrograde movement. At an order from
Robur the engineer reversed the engine, and the air-ship,
to use a naval expression, began to fall astern.

Every one was preparing to unship the propeller, when
George Kerns was surprised by a singular odor.

It was the gas from the burning fuse, which had accumulated in the chest, and was now escaping from the
fugitives' cabin. The foreman uttered an exclamation of
surprise.

"What is the matter?" inquired Robur.

"Can you smell anything? It seems to me that powder
is burning."

"Impossible, George."

"And the odor comes from the last cabin."

"What, their cabin?"

"Yes; can these wretches have set fire to the air-ship?"

"If it was only fire," cried Robur. "Quick, George, break in the door."

But the foreman had not time to take another step before a formidable explosion shook the "Albatross." The cabins were blown to pieces. The electric current was broken, the lights went out, and the air-ship was plunged into darkness. The larger part of the suspensive screws, twisted and broken, were disabled; but a few of the screws at the bow still maintained their rotary motion. Suddenly the deck parted just behind the turret inclosing the machinery of the forward propeller, and the after part of the deck fell off into space. Almost at the same time the suspensive screws stopped working and the wreck of the "Albatross" plunged down toward the sea. It meant a fall of nine thousand feet for the eight men who clung like shipwrecked sailors to the wreck.

The fall would have been rapid had it not been for the fact that the forward propeller had been jammed to a vertical position and was still revolving. Robur, with extraordinary coolness, had reached the shattered turret, seized the lever and changed the direction of the screw, which from propulsive had become suspensive.

This action did not arrest the fall, but it retarded it to such an extent that there was now no danger of asphyxia through a rapid fall through the air.

Eighty seconds after the explosion all that remained of the "Albatross" was ingulfed in the sea.

CHAPTER XVII.

IN WHICH WE MUST GO BACK TWO MONTHS.

THE morning after the 13th of June, that memorable night of the stormy meeting of the Weldon Club, an indescribable sensation startled the population of Philadelphia.

At the early hours of the morning even, the conversations taking place in the city all bore wholly on the unexpected and scandalous incident of the previous evening.

An intruder calling himself an inventor, claiming the strange title of Robur the Conqueror, a person of unknown origin and nationality, had presented himself at their meeting, insulted and ridiculed the balloonists, laughed at their faith in dirigible balloons, succeeded in raising an extraordinary tumult, and provoked threats which he finished by turning against his adversaries. At last, quitting the hall under cover of the smoking revolvers, he had disappeared, and in spite of the most careful searches could not be found.

The excitement was increased to a still higher pitch when it was found that since the 13th of June the president and secretary of the Weldon Club were missing. The night before they had left their club at their customary hour and had not been seen since.

Not only had these two important Philadelphians completely disappeared, but the valet Frycollin had also vanished. The incident made the valet the most celebrated member of his race, and never were Soulouque, Touissant L'Ouverture or Dessaline more talked of.

The following day, no news. Neither the two colleagues nor Frycollin made an appearance. The dismay increased. Large crowds surrounded the telegraph offices, anxiously seeking news of the missing men. Still nothing.

Nevertheless they but a few nights ago had left the club, and when last seen were starting out Walnut Street, arguing in loud tones, and followed by Frycollin.

Jem Cip, the vegetarian, had shaken the president's right hand, saying·

"Until to-morrow."

William T. Forbes had received a hearty clasp from Phil Evans, who said as he parted:

"*Au revoir*. I will see you in the morning."

Miss Dolly and Miss Mattie Forbes, so attached to Uncle Prudent, were in tears over his absence, and refused to be comforted. Three, four, five, six days passed; then a week, two weeks—no clew, no news regarding the absent citizens.

The most minute searches were made through the neighborhood. Nothing. The wharves and outgoing vessels were investigated. Nothing.

Fairmount Park was searched through and through. Nothing. Always nothing.

They noticed that the grass and shrubbery of the clearing had been beaten down, but could offer no explanation of the fact. In the fringe of trees surrounding the clearing, traces of a struggle were detected.

6

Had the two colleagues and the valet wandered into that portion of the park and been attacked by highwaymen or footpads? It was possible.

The police commenced to investigate the case, moving with traditional caution, slowness and stupidity. The Schuylkill was dragged and the shrubbery on its banks cut down. The search was futile, but the labor was not lost, as the Schuylkill was in sore need of a good work of cleaning.

The newspapers were appealed to. Advertisements, personals and descriptions filled all the papers, Democratic or Republican. The "Daily Negro," the organ of its race, published a portrait of Frycollin, taken from his last photograph. Rewards were offered to those who would give any news of the absentees and even to those who would find any clew that might lead to their discovery.

"Five thousand dollars to any one who—"

But no one claimed it, and the money remained in the treasury of the Weldon Club.

"Lost! Lost!! Lost!!! Uncle Prudent and Phil Evans, of Philadelphia."

The club was thrown into a state of confusion through the disappearance of its president and secretary. All work relating to the construction of their balloon, the "Go-ahead," was indefinitely suspended. The members of the club would entertain no proposition as to completing an enterprise during the absence of the principal promoters of the affair, and who had devoted a large part of their time and fortunes to the enterprise. Just at this time fresh news began to pour in relating to the strange phenomenon

which for some weeks past had defied all attempts at explanation.

Certainly no one yet dreamed of establishing any con-
nection between its singular reappearance and the no less
inexplicable disappearance of the two members of the
Weldon Club. It would have required an extraordinary
stretch of imagination to in any way connect the two facts.
But be this as it may, the asteroid, meteor or aerial monster, call it what you will, had been sighted under conditions which permitted the observers to better appreciate
its size and shape.

First in Canada, over the provinces of Ottawa and
Quebec, the morning after the disappearance of the Philadelphians; then a short time later it was seen in the west,
where it waged a trial of speed against the fastest trains on
the Pacific Railroad.

From this time out the doubts of the scientific world
were solved. The body was not a product of nature, it
was a flying machine based on a practical application of
the theory of the " heavier than air." If the inventor and
master of the air-ship wished to still preserve a personal incognito, he evidently was no longer desirous of keeping the
machine a secret, for on several occasions he had descended
close to the earth.

As regarded the mechanical powers of the machine, and
the engines supplying it with motive power, nothing was
as yet learned. At all events, the supposed meteor was
now firmly established to be a machine of aerial locomotion, possessing enormous powers of speed.

It had been sighted over the Celestial Empire, a little

later over Hindostan, and a few days after over the immense steppes of Russia.

Who was this powerful inventor who possessed such wonderful powers of locomotion and for whom there existed neither limit nor frontiers. Could it be the strange Robur, who had so brutally flung his theories down on the table of the Weldon Club?

Perhaps some bright minds were already divining this fact, but no one dreamed of advancing it in explanation of the disappearance of the president and secretary of the Weldon Club.

Matters were in this state when a dispatch arrived from Paris, by way of New York, reaching there thirty-seven minutes past eleven on the morning of July 6.

The dispatch contained the text of a document, which was inclosed in a snuff-box found in the streets of Paris, and which disclosed the fate of the absentees.

The author of the outrage was that Robur, who had come to Philadelphia to overthrow the theories of the balloonists. It was he who commanded the " Albatross," and who had dared to kidnap two Philadelphians. And now, unless they could construct an engine capable of successfully coping with the powerful air-ship, their colleagues were lost, and the Weldon Club robbed of its two most influential members. The telegram from Paris was addressed to the Weldon Club, and the members were at once notified of its contents.

Ten minutes later all Philadelphia had received the news, and within an hour it had been flashed over every wire throughout the entire United States. Many were inclined to view the pretended discovery with distrust. Some pronounced the telegram a forgery; others that it was an ill-timed joke, and others laid the responsibility on some enterprising reporter at a loss for a sensation. How could such an event transpire secretly within the well-regulated city of Philadelphia? How could the "Albatross" alight unobserved into Fairmount Park?

Very well. The incredulous still had the right to doubt, but their triumph was short-lived. They were deprived of their right seven days after the arrival of the telegram. The 13th of July the French packet "Normandie" entered the waters of New York Bay, and it brought with it the famous snuff-box. A special train carried the box in all haste to Philadelphia.

It was the snuff-box belonging to the president of the Weldon Club.

Jem Cip was obliged that day to resort to more substantial nourishment, for he nearly fainted at the sight of the familiar object. How many times had he borrowed the contents. It was immediately recognized by William T. Forbes, Bat Fyn, J. O. Tombler and the other members of the club, who had hundreds of times seen it open and shut beneath the hands of their venerated president. In short, the box was identified by every friend possessed by Uncle Prudent within the good city of Philadelphia, whose name indicates—without it being necessary to repeat the fact—that all the inhabitants love each other like brothers.

Not a shadow of doubt surrounded the mystery now. The most incredulous were silenced, not only by the

snuff-box of the president, but by the writing on the
paper as well. Desperate hands were shaken toward the
sky. Uncle Prudent and his colleague carried away by a
flying machine and their fellow-citizens unable to offer the
least means of assistance.

The Niagara Falls Company, of which Uncle Prudent
was the largest stockholder, was about to suspend and stop
their works. The Walton Watch Company, now that it
had lost its director, Phil Evans, was considering the
necessity of closing its factories.

In the meantime, after passing over Paris, all traces of
the "Albatross" had disappeared. Some hours later it had
been sighted for an instant over Rome, but that was all.
It had certainly been observed over Timbuctoo, but the
astronomers of that celebrated city—if there were any—
had not time as yet to send the result of their observations
to Europe.

As to the King of Dahomey, he would rather have cut
off the heads of twenty thousand of his subjects, and in-
cluded all his cabinet ministers in the lot than to tell the
result of his experience with flying machines. He had a
certain amount of dignity and prestige to preserve.

The 28th of September a rumor ran through the city
that Uncle Prudent and Phil Evans had been seen that
afternoon entering the residence of the president of the
Weldon Club, and, what is more extraordinary, the rumor
proved to be true.

Frycollin himself had been recognized, and the report
was thus verified.

An enthusiastic crowd, composed of the members of the club and their friends, were massed before Uncle Prudent's house, filling the air with a thousand hurrahs.

Jem Cip, having abandoned his dinner—vegetable soup and lettuce—was there, directly behind William T. Forbes and his two daughters, Miss Doll and Miss Mat. If Uncle Prudent had been a Mormon, he could have had for the asking two charming wives.

That evening the Weldon Club was to hold its monthly meeting, and as it was expected that the two colleagues would occupy their old places, the members counted on obtaining the history of their adventures. For some reason the returned men had maintained strict silence as to the events which had transpired during their sojourn on the "Albatross." Part of that which the two colleagues had not revealed, and had no desire to reveal is already known to us. We have learned of the audacious escape of the president and secretary during the night of July 27, their discovery by Robur, the wounding of Phil Evans by a shot from George Kerns's rifle, the cutting of the cable, and the "Albatross," deprived of the use of its propellers, carried away by a south-west wind.

The fugitives could follow its course by the electric lights on board, but in a short time it disappeared entirely. The fugitives had nothing to fear, as they deemed it impossible for Robur to return against the wind without the aid of his propellers in less than four hours.

Before that time, the "Albatross," destroyed by the explosion, would be a shattered wreck floating on the surface of the sea, the bodies of its commander and crew scattered

in every direction. The act of vengeance would be accomplished in all its horror.

Uncle Prudent and Phil Evans, considering it as but a
case of legitimate defense, were not troubled with remorse.

Phil Evans had been wounded but slightly by the bullet
from the air-ship, and, there being no further need of delay, the three men proceeded along the coast, with the
hope of meeting some inhabitants. Their hopes were realized. The western side of Chatham Island was inhabited
by about a hundred natives, who lived by hunting and fishing. The approach of the air-ship had been detected by
the savages, who fled in dismay at the sight. They took
the fugitives for supernatural beings, and worshiped them.

Frycollin, as a black spirit, received the most humble
adoration and apparently enjoyed the position remarkably
well. As was expected by Uncle Prudent and Phil Evans,
the air-ship did not return. They concluded that the explosion had occurred while the " Albatross " was high in
the air, and from that time they ceased to speak of the inventor and his remarkable machine. They waited now for
an opportunity to regain the United States. Chatham
Island is frequented but little by navigators, and the month
of August passed, leaving the fugitives to ask themselves
whether they had not only exchanged one prison for another.

At last, on the 3d of September, a vessel stopped at the
island to take in a fresh supply of water.

It will be remembered that at the time of capture in
Fairmount Park, Uncle Prudent had on his person several
thousand dollars in bank-notes—more than sufficient te
pay their way back to America.

After taking an affectionate leave of the natives, who overpowered them with demonstrations of the highest respect, Uncle Prudent, Phil Evans, and Frycollin embarked for Auckland, and in two days arrived at the capital of New Zealand. There they took passage on a Pacific packet, and on September 20, after a pleasant trip, the survivors of the "Albatross" reached San Francisco.

Taking the first train leaving the city over the Pacific Railroad, Uncle Prudent, his colleague, and the valet Frycollin, started on the long stretch for home. On the 28th, they arrived at Philadelphia. This is a complete record of their movements since their escape and after leaving Chatham Island. This is how the president and secretary were enabled to take their old places that night at the meeting of the Weldon Club.

After the first salvos of hurrahs had swept over the meeting, leaving the two colleagues calm and unconcerned, Uncle Prudent took off his hat and rose to his feet.

"Gentlemen, the meeting is opened."

Frenzied shouts rose up, and they were permissible, for if there was nothing extraordinary in the fact that the meeting was opened, there was at least in the fact that it had been opened by Uncle Prudent, assisted by Phil Evans. The president waited for the tumult to subside, and then continued:

"At our last meeting, gentlemen, there was considerable discussion (Hear, hear!) between the partisans of the forward propeller and those of the rear propeller for our balloon, the 'Go-ahead.' (Expressions of surprise.) Since then we have found means to restore harmony between the frontites and the rearites, and that means is to have two propellers, one at each end." (Silence and general stupefaction.)

And this was all. Yes, all. Of the kidnappings of the president and secretary of the Weldon Club, not a word. Not a word of the "Albatross" or the inventor, Robur. Not a word of the voyage or the means by which the prisoners had escaped. Not a word as to the fate of the "Albatross." The balloonists would certainly have questioned their colleagues, but they maintained such a serious and reserved demeanor that all curiosity was warned off.

Uncle Prudent, taking advantage of the silence which filled the room, continued:

"Gentlemen, nothing remains but to complete the work on the 'Go-ahead' and start on our conquest of the air. The meeting is adjourned."

CHAPTER XVIII.

ENDING THE AUTHENTIC HISTORY OF THE "ALBATROSS."

THE 29th of April of the following year, seven months after the unexpected return of Uncle Prudent and Phil Evans, there was a considerable stir in the good city of Philadelphia. The balloon "Go-ahead," completed through the enterprise of the Weldon Club, was at last ready to take possession of its natural element. The celebrated Harry W. Tinder was engaged to manage the balloon. The passengers were to be the president and secretary of the Weldon Club.

The "Go-ahead" possessed all the qualities that a balloon should have.

Its volume permitted it to rise to the highest point attainable by balloons; its impermeability furnished it with the power to maintain itself in the atmosphere for an indefinite length of time; its solidity to brave the dilation of the gas and the violence of the wind and rain; its capacity to gain an ascensional power sufficient to raise with all its accessories an electrical machine which was to communicate the motive power to the propellers.

The balloon was of an elongated form, which facilitated horizontal speed. The car, shaped like that of Captains Krebs and Renard, carried the supplies necessary for aerostatics, instruments, cables, anchors, guide-ropes, and the electric batteries and accumulators. The car was furnished in front with a propeller, and at the other end with a propeller and governor.

After being inflated the "Go-ahead" was transported to the clearing in Fairmount Park, the very spot where the air-ship had alighted.

The morning of the 20th of April, everything was ready.

At eleven o'clock the enormous balloon was tugging at the ropes, anxious to take its first flight into space.

The weather was admirably suited to the trial, unless, perhaps, some desired a stiffer breeze, so that the proof would be more conclusive. No one ever denied the possibility of steering balloons through a calm atmosphere, but to do so in a current of wind is another matter.

But, on this day, there was neither wind nor the signs of

any, and a better time could not have been chosen for a successful aerial trial.

Is it necessary to speak of the immense crowd that had gathered in Fairmount Park, of the many trains which emptied into Philadelphia the curious multitude from neighboring states, of the suspension of · industrial and commercial life, to enable all to assist at the spectacle—employers, employés, men, women, and children, congressmen, soldiers, magistrates, reporters, inhabitants, white and black, all gathered in the vast clearing? Is it necessary to describe the burning emotions of the populace, the sudden movements and impulses of the crowd? Must we number the hip-hips that sounded from every Quaker when Uncle Prudent and Phil Evans appeared over the side of the car, that was draped with the American colors?

Must we admit that the larger number of the curious ones below had been attracted, not by the "Go-ahead," but to see these two extraordinary men who had spent so long a time in the air? But why two and not three? Why not Frycollin? Frycollin found the cruise of the "Albatross" sufficient glory for him, and had declined the honor of accompanying his master on the "Go-ahead." He came in for no share of the acclamations which fell around the president and secretary of the Weldon Club. It goes without saying that the members of that illustrious body were all in conspicuous places reserved for them within the circle of ropes.

J. O. Tombler, Bat Fyn, William T. Forbes, with Miss Doll and Miss Mat on each arm, all had gathered there to affirm by their presence that nothing could ever separate the partisans of the "lighter than air."

At 11:20, the report of a cannon announced the completion of the final details.

The "Go-ahead" now waited the next signal.

A second report sounded at 11:25. The "Go-ahead," held by the ropes, was swinging some fifteen or twenty yards above the clearing.

Uncle Prudent and Phil Evans, standing in the forward part of the car, each placed their right hands on their bosoms, which signified that their hearts were with the enterprise. Then they extended their left hands toward the zenith, which signified that the largest balloon ever built was about to take possession of the superterrestrial domain. One hundred thousand hands pressed themselves to one hundred thousand bosoms, and one hundred thousand others pointed toward the heavens. A third cannon-shot sounded at 11:30.

"Let go all," cried Uncle Prudent. And the "Go-ahead" arose "majestically"—adverb consecrated by long usage in aerostatic descriptions. It was, in truth, a superb spectacle. The launching of a vessel on an aerial sea

The "Go-ahead" ascended rapidly, following a direct vertical line—a proof of the absolute calm of the atmosphere—and stopped at a height of 750 feet. There commenced a series of horizontal maneuvers. The "Go-ahead," driven by its propellers, darted toward the sun at a speed of about thirty feet a second, the speed of the whale through the sea. A fresh salvo of hurrahs reached the clever aeronauts.

Then, under the action of the rudder, the "Go-ahead" began to execute circular evolutions and oblique cuts, obeying and following every move of the hand of the steersman. It turned sharply in a restricted circle, darted to the front, and then to the rear, convincing even the most stubborn opponents of dirigible ballooning. It was to be regretted that the wind was calm during the trial. One could have seen the "Go-ahead" execute without hesitation all the movements of aerial navigation, tacking or crossing the currents of air as easily as a steamship.

At this moment the balloon ascended some hundred yards higher.

The maneuver was understood by the crowd below. Uncle Prudent and his companion were endeavoring to find a current of air, in order to complete the proof.

The "Go-ahead" ascended in a vertical line, its enormous dimensions gradually decreasing in size to those beneath. This fact did not lessen the curiosity of the spectators who were still straining their eyes to follow the movements of the balloon.

The ascensional movement was continued until the "Go-ahead" reached a height of 12,000 feet. The sky was so clear and cloudless that it was still visible to the watchers below.

It was now directly over the clearing, as if it had been attached by a rope. Not a breath of wind stirred, and the balloon was steered without encountering the slightest resistance.

Suddenly a cry raised itself from the crowd, a cry projected by a hundred thousand voices. Every arm was extended to the north-west, toward a point in the horizon.

There in the depths of azure appeared a moving body which grew larger as it approached.

Was it a bird beating with its wings its way through the high regions of space, or was it a meteor coming obliquely through the atmosphere? In any case, it had the power of excessive speed and rapidly approached the scene.

A suspicion, which was communicated to every brain, ran through the crowd.

The " Go-ahead " had evidently sighted the strange object, for it headed toward the east with increased speed. Yes, the crowd had comprehended. A name, uttered by one of the members of the Weldon Club, was repeated by thousands of tongues.

" The ' Albatross!' the ' Albatross!' " It was the " Albatross." It was Robur reappearing in the heights of the heavens, and who, like a gigantic bird of prey, seemed ready to leap on the " Go-ahead." And yet, nine months ago, the air-ship had been destroyed by the explosion, its screws broken and the deck cut in two. Had it not been for the extraordinary coolness of the inventor, who had changed the gyratory motion of the propulsive screw and turned it into a suspension screw, the *personnel* of the crew would have been asphyxiated by the rapidity of the fall. But if they escaped that phase of the danger, how was it that they were not drowned in the waters of the Pacific.

The *débris* of the deck, the branches of the propellers,

the walls of the cabins, all that remained of the "Albatross," formed a wreck which still floated.

The wounded bird had fallen to the water, but its wings still supported it above the surface of the ocean. For some hours Robur and his men remained on board the wreck and resigned themselves to their fate.

Providence, as it is styled by those who believe in Divine intervention in human affairs—chance for those who do not believe in Providence—came to the aid of the castaways. Several hours after day-break they were perceived by a passing vessel, which sent a boat to their assistance. The vessel took up not only Robur and his companions, but the *débris* of the air-ship as well.

The inventor contented himself with saying that his vessel had perished in a collision, and his incognito was respected. The ship was an English three-master, the "Two Friends," of Liverpool. Its destination was Melbourne, which it reached some days after. They were now in Australia, but still far from Island X, to which place it was necessary that they return as early as possible.

Among the wreck the inventor had found in the *débris* of the forward cabin a considerable sum of money, which served every need of his companions.

A short time after his arrival at Melbourne, he purchased a small schooner of about 100 tons burden, and quickly regained Island X.

Robur was now possessed with but a single idea—vengeance. But to revenge himself, it was necessary to construct a second "Albatross," after all an easy work for he who had built the first. He utilized in the work whatever portions of the old air-ship that were available, and in eight months the work was finished, and a new "Albatross," similar to the one destroyed by the explosion, as powerful and as rapid, was ready for flight.

The same machine, and the same crew, and when it is understood that that crew was filled with rage toward Uncle Prudent and Phil Evans in particular, and the Weldon Club in general, the situation will be comprehended.

The "Albatross" left Island X during the first days of April. During the trip, as Robur desired to remain unobserved, the larger part of the flight was made behind the clouds. Arrived over North America, the machine descended in a deserted portion of the West. There the inventor, preserving the strictest incognito, kept himself informed of every event transpiring within the city of Philadelphia, and soon had the pleasure of learning that the Weldon Club was ready to commence its experiments, that the "Go-ahead," bearing Uncle Prudent and Phil Evans, would leave Philadelphia April 29.

This was the opportunity for Robur and his crew to satisfy the vengeance that filled their hearts. A terrible vengeance from which the "Go-ahead" would not escape. A public vengeance, which at the same time would prove the superiority of the air-ship over balloons and other apparatus of the kind.

That is why the air-ship, like a huge vulture, was hovering over Fairmount Park.

Yes! it was the "Albatross," easily recognized, even by those who had never seen it.

The "Go-ahead" was still fleeing. But it understood

the fact that it was useless to attempt to escape in a horizontal line.   It therefore sought a vertical flight, not by
approaching the earth, for the air-ship would have
barred the way, but by rising still higher in the air.   It
was very audacious, but it was their only chance.

In the meanwhile the " Albatross " began to rise also.
Being much smaller than the " Go-ahead," it looked like
a sword-fish attacking a whale.   In some minutes the balloon had risen to some 15,000 feet, while the " Albatross "
closely followed in the ascensional track, and reaching the
" Go-ahead," circled round it, drawing nearer at every
turn.

It could have annihilated it at a single blow by piercing
the covering of the balloon.   Then Uncle Prudent and
his companions would have been crushed by a frightful
fall.

The crowd stood breathless, mute with horror, seized
with that fright which oppresses the chest and turns the
head at seeing a person fall from a great height.   An
aerial combat was about to transpire, a combat which did
not offer one half of the chances for safety presented by a
naval combat.

The " Go-ahead " was draped with the American colors,
to which Robur replied by hoisting the black flag with the
golden sun of Robur the Conqueror.   The " Go-ahead "
was endeavoring to distance its enemy by rising still higher
in the air, throwing out every pound of ballast, and adding
3,000 feet to its height.   The " Albatross," its propellers
working at full speed, was following every movement of
the balloon.

Suddenly a cry of horror was raised from the cloud. The "Go-ahead" was increasing in size and the air-ship was lowering rapidly. This time it was a fall. The gas, dilating in the higher zones of the air, had burst the covering, and, half-empty, the balloon was rapidly falling.

But the air-ship, moderating its suspensive screws, was dropping with equal speed, and when about 3,600 feet above the earth reached the car of the balloon. The maneuver was so accurately performed that the passengers might have stepped to the deck of the air-ship.

Uncle Prudent and Phil Evans would have refused Robur's assistance, would have refused to be saved by him, but the crew of the air-ship cast themselves on the passengers and forcibly compelled them to pass from the "Go-ahead" to the "Albatross."

Then the air-ship disengaged itself and remained stationary, while the balloon, emptied of gas, fell on the park trees and swayed with the wind.

Complete silence reigned below. It seemed as if life had been suspended in every bosom. Many eyes were already closed to shut out the sight of the catastrophe.

Uncle Prudent and Phil Evans were again the prisoners of the inventor, Robur, and now that they were retaken, would he again carry them into space, doomed to perpetual imprisonment.

We must wait and see. In the meantime, instead of remounting into the air, the "Albatross" drew closer to the earth, as if it wished to alight. The crowd cleared a space in the middle of the clearing.

The "Albatross" stopped within two yards of the

earth. Then in the midst of the profound silence the voice of the inventor was heard:

"Citizens of the United States, the president and sec-retary of the Weldon Club are again in my power. In capturing and keeping them I would only be exercising my right of reprisal. But the passion raised in their hearts by the success of the 'Albatross' assures me that the state of mind is not ready for that important revolution which will one day accomplish the conquest of the air. Uncle Pru-dent and Phil Evans, you are free."

The president, secretary, the aeronaut and his assistant had only to step to the ground. The "Albatross" re-mounted to about forty feet above the crowd and Robur continued:

"Citizens of the United States, my task is for the pres-ent finished. My experiment is premature. Science should not precede the mental capacity of the times. There should be evolution, not revolution. I have come too soon and find that the time is not yet ripe for my work. I therefore take leave of you, and I bear my secret with me. But it will not be lost to humanity. It will be found when the world is wise enough to profit by it and prudent enough never to abuse it. Citizens of the United States, adieu!"

And the "Albatross," beating the air with its seventy-four screws, and carried off by its two propellers, disap-peared in the east in the midst of a tempest of hurrahs, which this time were of admiration. The two colleagues were profoundly humiliated through the exposure of what they had endeavored to keep secret, while the changeable

crowd which a short time previous had shouted their admiration, now changed their cheers to sarcastic jeers.

*   *   *   *   *   *   *

And now that same question, " Who is this Robur?"

Robur is the science of the future, perhaps that of to
morrow.

The future of aerial locomotion belongs to the air-ship
and not to the balloon, and it is for the " Albatross
that the conquest of the air is definitely reserved.

THE END.